CW00704720

Time Enough for the World to End

David Viner

Viva Djinn (Horde) Publishing

Published by
Viva Djinn (Horde) Publishing
Norwich, UK

www.vivadjinn.com

ISBN: 978-1-913873-04-2

All stories and this collection Copyright ©2021 David Viner.

All rights reserved. No part of this publication may be reproduced, stored in a retrieval system, or transmitted, in any form or by any means without the prior permission in writing of the publisher.

All characters in this book are fictitious, and any resemblance to actual persons, living or dead, is purely coincidental.

This book is sold subject to the condition that it shall not, by way of trade or otherwise, be lent, resold, hired out or otherwise circulated without the publisher's prior consent in any form other than that supplied by the publisher.

British Library Cataloguing in Publication Data available.

Design and layout: David Viner

Original Cover Photography from Unsplash by Marten Bjork

Contents

Introduction

After reading *Underneath the Arches* and *Jumper* several people said to me, "Oh, you've obviously based them on the *The Time Traveler's Wife.*"

Actually, when I wrote those stories, whose first drafts appeared in 2006 and 2011 respectively, I had only vaguely heard of the novel by Audrey Niffenegger, but had definitely never read it. It was only when I saw the film a few years ago and then finally read the book in 2019 that I could see why the commenters made that connection.

But, no, the stories in this collection hadn't been influenced by that book – the sources of my interest in both time travel and science fiction occurred many years before that novel was written. Reading Dan Dare in the Eagle comic and watching TV programmes such as Doctor Who, Timeslip and Space Patrol in the 1960/70s were early influences upon me, as was reading H. G. Wells' *The Time Machine* before I was 12. Books by John Wyndham such as *The Day of the Triffids* and *The Kraken Wakes* introduced me to the 'Great British Disaster Novel' genre, which also includes such gems as *All Fools Day* by Edmund Cooper and John Christopher's *The Death of Grass*. These were all absorbed by my growing mind while I was still in my teens and early twenties, alongside other favourites such as Michael Moorcock, Isaac Asimov, Robert Heinlein, Edmund Cooper, Brian Aldiss and Christopher Priest, amongst others.

Small wonder that, once I'd started penning my own stories, there would be a proliferation of time travel and 'world ending' tales.

This collection of short stories, written over the past twenty years, dips into both of those themes, and some of the entries here contain elements of both.

I hope you enjoy them.

David Viner, November 2021

The Sweeper

With precise twitches of the brush, Jonathan sweeps the yard.

Just before she went shopping his mother asked him to clean the yard. Jonathan is a good boy and always does as he is told.

Gripping the broom in stick-thin fingers, he dances the dust and debris into the corner where the fence and wall don't quite meet. Then he flicks it through the gap and out into the alleyway beyond.

Tomorrow there will be more dust and debris, and Jonathan will again sweep it all up and poke it through the hole. Jonathan has been sweeping dust for a long time now. As he works he ponders over what's out in the alleyway, other than the dust and debris, of course. Since his mother went shopping he hasn't heard anyone walk along it. Momentarily, he is curious about where the people went, but then there is always more dust and debris to sweep up, and he goes about the business of persuading it first into the corner and then out through the hole with scrupulous accuracy. In fact, as meticulous as his mother had always been – he'd inherited that much, at least.

In between the sweeping Jonathan makes a cup of tea. It's cold and tastes dusty, it always does. It doesn't, however, taste of tea. Not surprising since Jonathan used the last of the tea bags some time ago. There isn't any milk or sugar either, and the kettle no longer makes the water hot.

He looks up from his sweeping. Another deep red sunset shot through with purples and blues and greys. He thinks, not for the first time, "The sky has been amazing since mother went shopping."

He wonders when she will be back.

The Sweeper *was an exercise in writing a tiny story with hints of a larger one buried inside it. The version here was written in 2010 although, in 2012, a much shorter version won an online 101-word competition run via Facebook by Colors of my Soul:*

https://www.facebook.com/notes/3138326792938610/

I have been a member of the Redwell Writers writing group since its inception back in 2006 when local writer Andrew Hook (andrew-hook.com) first started it. He introduced the group to the "Character/Scene/Conflict" method of producing prompts for writing exercises. The following story, **The Wife Hunt,** *came about in 2015 through this exercise. See the following link for the full details of this exercise:*

https://www.vivadjinn.com/writingexercise.html

The Wife Hunt

His footfalls echo back from the glass fronts of the shops. As he passes, he eyes his reflection. Unaware of how wrong he might be, he imagines he fits in.

He advances into the shopping centre. Sometimes, he even examines what the shops contain. He sees a newsagent as closed as the rest. It's Sunday, therefore it is correct that they would be shut. He peers through the newsagent's door. Inside, the gloom hides much of the interior but, close to the other side of the door, he can see a stand sparsely populated with papers and comics. His eyes flick over a few of the nearer titles – a Sunday Graphic paper has been stuck incongruously next to a Beano and an Eagle, the latter with Dan Dare on the cover in a story called 'Prisoners of Space.'

The lies we told ourselves, he thinks, removing his attention from the newsagent and investigating the haberdashery a few doors away. "This is more like it," he mumbles.

The door is locked, as expected. He inserts a key in the lock and holds it still while it analyses the configuration. Seconds later, there is a click and he pushes the door open.

It is as unlike his own shop as it could possibly be, so different compared to previous experiences. Here, the shelves of materials, fabrics, cottons and sewing implements are openly exposed. He marvels at the trust the proprietors exhibit. He cannot understand how such a thing could ever exist. But, amongst the neatness of the displays, there is an area of untidiness, as if someone has been searching for something. Stepping fully into the shop he sniffs the atmosphere. There is a scent, one he recognises. She has been here, without a doubt. However, the devices within his nostrils also reveal that she left at least thirty minutes previously. He may already be too late.

He closes the door again, noting how the lock clicks back into place. Feeling in a pocket, he pulls out the glasses, placing them on the bridge of his nose. The view of the shopping centre changes – several ethereal traces can be seen, including his own, which is the strongest. Smaller traces lace across his, no doubt those of insects, probably flies and moths. Another large but fainter trace is still detectable. It appears to start within the haberdashery and leads off to a side door.

He follows.

The door, once it is unlocked, takes him out into low, weak sunshine. The glasses are useless in this light, meagre though it is. Also, they are anachronistic – a giveaway. He removes them, though not before detecting one last trace image that suggests she turned left, towards the sea. He also unclips the devices from his nostrils – out here the smell of the sea and other pollutants are too much for their sensitive receptors.

The noise of the sea grows in his ears. Seagulls circle in the air, their cries adding to the sound of the crashing water. The railings of the promenade prevent direct access to the beach, about ten feet below. There is no sand, rounded pebbles stretch from the concrete wall out to where waves hit them, some two hundred feet away. Not too far to his left a set of steps lead down to the pebbles. Half way from the steps to the sea a lone figure sits, gazing off towards the horizon.

His feet crunch the stones underfoot as he makes his way towards the woman. She leaves it to the last moment before turning her head to face him. He dare not come any closer.

"You're too late," she says, without emotion.

Beside her are seven lengths of cloth. She has overlaid a large paisley patterned material with six narrow strips of grey weave. Strands of cotton appear randomly scattered over them. They do not stir, although there is a breeze. He recognises the arrangement; the positioning is not random. It has power. What she can do easily with things to hand, he can only achieve with difficulty through technology.

"Why did you leave?" he asks.

"You really need to ask that?" This time her voice holds a sneer.

"Why the 1950s?"

"It was convenient," she replies, back to the unemotional. "It had what I needed."

He steps in front of her, directly between her and the sea.

Her right hand casually moves one of the grey strips of cloth and the stones upon which he is standing start to slip. He steps to one side, and watches pebbles tumble down towards the waves.

"I know about him," he says.

"As if I care," she replies.

"Is that true?"

She glances up at him, face drawn. She has been crying.

"I have dissolved the contract. You will be receiving notice from my solicitor," she adds.

She returns her attention to the cloth, one hand smoothing out a crease in the paisley. He knows it is almost ready.

"You were always too clever for me," he states.

"You held me back. Not any more."

A pale green belt is placed over the grey strips and her outline wavers. She is activating it and he cannot interfere.

"Will I see you again?" he asks.

She shakes her head and leaves. He is left alone with just the pebbles and the noise of waves crashing for company. His technology cannot analyse her route this time. It barely had the power to lead him here.

A couple stand on the promenade watching him. He wonders how much they have seen. In his pocket one hand finds the most complex device – that which brought him here. He locates his fingers at the appropriate points on its surface and waves at the couple on the promenade with his other hand. Hesitantly, they wave back.

He applies pressure to the device and returns home.

Bugger the Consequences

I've always had trouble keeping my trap shut. But, this time, there were definitely mitigating circumstances. Well, that's my excuse, anyway.

The 'mitigating circumstances' in this case were the mice. Thousands, if not millions of the little bastards. Okay, so we've had plagues of them in New South Wales before, but not like this. On a bad night you might have had to kill a hundred of the little buggers but that was peanuts to what I was facing last night.

We'd tried poison, traps, tanks of water to drown them in, electric wires and God knows what else – but still they came. Then, not long before midnight, while I'd been trying to stop their mates from invading the grain silo, some of them had chewed through a cable somewhere and the whole farm was plunged into darkness.

Charlene had had enough. In a panic, she woke the kids and herded them into the car to take them off to her mother's in Maitland, leaving me defending our livelihood.

And a fat lot of good my defending was doing us. Several hours later the grain was unsalvageable, the chickens were nothing more than chewed bones, and the crops out in the fields stripped down to stubble. The damned mice were not only all over the farm, they were all over the house as well. They ran in the kitchen, in the lounge, up the stairs, in the bedrooms and had even managed to get up into the roof space. The place stunk of mice, and mice eating dead mice once they'd run out of normal stuff to eat. I even saw live mice taking bites out of each other.

In my frustration I was reduced to pulverising as many of them as I could with a spade while they ran around my feet. Each hit took out more than a dozen but that didn't stop more taking their place.

I was doing exactly that when the stranger arrived. A light entered the farm gate and after a muffled clunk, I heard him approach me from behind while I continued to splatter mice.

"Having a spot of trouble?" he asked. I couldn't place the accent; definitely not Australian, anyway. Possibly British – 'spot of trouble' was just the damned stupid thing a Brit would say.

"You ain't kidding," I replied.

There was no moon and the stars didn't give enough light for me to see the guy properly. Not that I really had time to look – a quick glance gave the impression he was short and thin, wearing some sort of one-piece thing. His head was large – crash helmet, I presumed, which also explained the one-piece – probably some sort of leathers. He certainly needed them with all the mice running around. I wore bicycle clips on my pants to make sure the little sods didn't climb up and nip me in the nadgers.

The stranger stood a few feet behind watching me battering mice into the dirt. In spite of the low light level I could make out the ground in front of me heaving with them.

"What's happening?" the stranger asked.

"Strewth! Can't you see the little bleeders? We're overrun with the bastards."

"A plague," he concluded.

"Yeah, an effing plague. Where have you been the last coupla days? It's been all over the radio and TV."

"And what are you doing about them?" he further enquired.

"What do you effing mean 'what am I doing about them'?" I replied. "I'm effing killing them, that's what I'm effing doing. I'm poisoning 'em, drowning 'em, trapping them and hitting them with this effing spade for all the good it does. I was electrocuting the little bleeders before they chewed through the wiring."

"Interesting," he said.

I stopped smacking mice and turned to face him.

"Interesting?" I shouted. "It's more than damned interesting. It's a bloody disaster."

My voice lowered and I almost sobbed. "There's just too many of them," I said. "They've eaten me chickens, stripped me fields and turned my stock into

8

more of themselves. I'm ruined, the whole effing farm is ruined."

"Your manner of rendering them deceased is not efficient, then?" the stranger asked.

"Look, who the bloody hell are you? Why the hell am I standing here talking to some idiot in a helmet when my livelihood's being reduced to nothing?"

The stranger, his face in complete darkness, pondered for a second.

"What would you like to do about them, then?"

"What?"

"What solution would be the best in such circumstances?"

"I want them dead. I want them all dead. Killed, slaughtered, eradicated, massacred, exterminated…"

"All of them?"

"Yeah, every last stinking mouse on the whole farm, the whole country, the whole effing planet."

"Even if there were environmental concerns if such an extermination took place?"

"I don't care – I just want them all dead." I was almost crying by this point.

"And that is your preferred solution for plagues?"

"What?"

"Your solution for such plagues is always extermination?"

"Too bloody right it is. Kill them all off, bugger the consequences."

"Hmm," he said. "Maybe it would be for the best."

I shook off several mice that were attempting to run up my trousers and the stranger turned away back to where he'd parked his bike. I watched him walk and it was a weird walk. His spindly legs didn't seem to work properly. Then I noticed that the mice avoided him, hurrying out of his path. I urgently needed to know how he was doing that.

I ran after him while reaching into my pocket for my torch. The battery was past its best but it could still produce a bit of light. I caught up to him before he reached his bike, though now I saw that it resembled no motorcycle I had ever encountered.

I grabbed his shoulder and spun him around. Shining the torch into his helmet I realised that he wasn't actually wearing a helmet. He wasn't wearing a one-piece either, though my eyes couldn't decide whether or not he was naked.

The enormous eyes in that gigantic head were pitch black. He gently pushed the torch away from his face with spindly fingers.

I stood there in shock. His mouth didn't move though I still heard him say.

"We will deal with your plague and, as you so indicated, we will 'bugger the consequences'."

He tapped me on the forehead, saying, "You will be tasked to observe."

He turned and mounted the vehicle.

I watched it skim the ground for a few yards before it lifted into the sky. Then, it shot off at great speed and, within seconds, was lost from view.

Playing the failing torchlight over the advancing mice showed me I had no chance of winning this war. With shaking hands I managed to get the truck started and, abandoning the farm, headed towards Maitland. But I couldn't get that face, those eyes out of my head.

I reached Maitland just as the sun came up. There were few people about. At least there were no mice here… yet.

But, before I could reach Charlene's mother's house, ships swarmed out of the skies, buzzing like a nest of angry wasps. They hit the far side of town first, where Charlene and the kids were. The beams coming out of the ships silently swept back and forth across the land.

I floored the accelerator. As I sped through town I saw people running from their houses, screaming. Anyone caught in a beam was instantly turned to dust though, somehow, I managed to avoid them.

At the house I screeched to a halt. The door was open and I ran inside. There was no one there. Back in the front garden I noticed five patches of dust littering the parched lawn.

Above me a small ship broke formation and the vehicle landed in the road. One of them stepped out and came up to me. I could do nothing other than stand there, mouth open.

"We have halted your plague and have buggered the consequences. Thank you for observing."

He returned to the ship and the skies became clear.

I slumped to the ground, sobbing. All around me was devoid of any human activity. I suspected the rest of the world would be the same.

A few hours later, as the sun began to set, I heard a familiar pattering noise. I sat up and watched a brown tide of mice engulfing the road. I lay down and with their feet running all over me, I waited for the end.

In 2021 Australia suffered yet another of its mouse plagues. **Bugger The Consequences** *was written in 2014, not long after a previous one. In 2020 the story was also entered into a Wattpad competition which had the theme of "Bizarre Apocalypse" where it was a joint winner.*

Underneath the Arches

The body was found encased up to its neck in cement. The flesh had not decomposed and was dry, as if some mummification process had been involved.

The hand-written note pinned to the head stated that the victim had arranged his own death, though no reason was given as to how or even why.

Dizziness subsides and I take stock of my new surroundings. Accompanied by the methodical clanketty-clank of metal wheel upon rail, the desert drifts past. Another train, I curse. Always trains. Why?

Through the uneven slats of the boxcar's walls, the pale moon slices up the inventory: three crates, their tops nailed down; obligatory bales of straw, four thereof; bundles of wood, several; one cask, tied to a slat to stop it tumbling. The cask is filled with long-handled tools that rattle with every rail joint we pass over. Losing interest I squint out into the night. American mid-west, I conjecture. Not a hard guess. When? Who cares. I probably won't be here long enough for it to matter.

Outside, the train's passage dislodges a tumbleweed from where it lay. Blowing in the wind, I think and quickly suppress the thought before it can take effect. I need a rest from this.

"Oh God," I cry. "Just give me a few hours – is it too much to ask?"

There's something warm in my hand. Oh yes, now I remember. I push the remains of the burger into my mouth, aware of the bristle of beard that needs trimming yet again. Chewing, I savour even the gristle that clings between my teeth. After licking ketchup from my fingers I lie down, exhausted as usual, and let the rhythm sway me into fitful sleep.

In the early dawn I wake and watch the desert lumber past. It is striped with extended shadows. I retrieve the water bottle from my pocket. A constant companion since I stole it, it is nearly empty and I drink half the remainder.

"What's up, Ali? You look like you've just seen a ghost."

"Bloody hell, Jenny," Alison said, collapsing into the chair at her desk, "I think I did. Damn it, I need a drink. Down at the burger stand near the tube station. This guy in front of me in the queue… he just… just…"

"What? He just… what?" Jenny said, bringing Alison a cup of cold water from the nearby dispenser.

"Disappeared into thin air. Just like that." Alison snapped her fingers to demonstrate, unaware of the water that splashed from the cup onto the papers on her desk.

Jenny frowned. "What did he look like?"

After Alison had described the man it was Jenny's turn to feel faint. She sat down.

The sound of Paul Hardcastle's N-N-N-Nineteen, the current number one, percolated through the office from an open window. Outside, in the blazing sunshine, a window cleaner whistled along to his radio while he soaped the glass.

But Jenny felt a chill run through her bones.

A raucous sound awakes me, which my ears identify as the wheezing of a steam locomotive. Opening my eyes, I see the woman seated opposite. A quick glance around shows me that she is the only other occupant of the compartment. She is tiny and encased from neck to floor in a black cloak. The equally dark bonnet enveloping most of her head reveals only a single sliver of silvery hair. I can imagine the scream that has just passed her still-open lips.

I sigh and, for some reason, glance at my watch trying to recall the song that had brought me here. The LCD display tells me it is the middle of the night in July – the sunshine streaking across the snow outside begs to differ. Through the mist I am sure I can just distinguish the outlines of hills or possibly mountains in the distance.

The woman whimpers. The coach does not possess a corridor so, until the train pulls into a station, she is trapped in here with me.

"I won't hurt you," I tell her but, obviously, she does not believe me. Above her head a wooden, brass-edged case bounces precariously on a luggage rack that appears to be constructed mainly of knotted string. Despite the lack of upholstering on the plank that purports to be a seat, I lie down and attempt a return to sleep.

Martin's task was to remove the body from the cement. He blew on his hands to warm them, the room being refrigerated to help preserve the corpse. The mist from his breath tumbled through the air before dissipating.

While he sorted out the tools, the drills and cutters he intended using for the job, he hummed Bridge Over Troubled Water – couldn't get the damned song out of his mind. At least, he thought, Simon and Garfunkel were preferable to Lee Marvin's recent, detestable Wandrin' Star – he'd had that one going through his head for far too many days.

Then he switched on his portable transistor radio. It was playing the Moody Blues who were singing Question.

"That's better," he mumbled and picked up his electric drill.

"Sorry, no," Linda said to the caller. "The place was empty when I moved in. If there was ever a Jenny here then she didn't leave a forwarding address."

The man groaned and hung up. Linda turned the TV on – Top of the Pops was showing the video to Madonna's current release, Into The Groove.

The first impression is of being crushed on all sides and then I sense the speed. Around me, bodies press against mine; I am unaccustomed to such closeness. As my eyes focus I see the shock of those around me and I recoil slightly as well. They are all oriental, Chinese or Japanese maybe. Outside, the scenery flashes past at speeds I have never previously experienced on the ground.

This is unnerving and I wonder which melody brought me here. The name of a band, the Vapours, pops into my head.

Not caring about the effect it will have on the other passengers, I deliberately hum another tune, and darkness once again enfolds me.

Jenny contacted the police a few hours after Stephen went missing. A barrage of questions followed, which she answered as best she could. As she spoke, the fingers of her right hand constantly twisted the engagement ring around the third finger of her left hand.

Yes, she had last talked to him by phone and, in the middle of the conversation – actually in the middle of a word, if she remembered correctly – he had suddenly stopped talking and she'd heard the phone drop. Yes, she'd hung up and tried ringing his number again, several times in fact, but the line remained engaged. In a panic she'd driven across London to his flat.

Letting herself in, she'd replaced the phone on its cradle and searched in vain. In the kitchen a half-eaten cheese sandwich, already beginning to curl, sat on a plate alongside a cold cup of tea. In the lounge the hi-fi, still turned on, had finished playing side one of an LP, Junk Culture by Orchestral Manoeuvres in the Dark, Stephen's latest acquisition. She recalled hearing the track, Locomotion, in the background when they were talking on the phone.

The policeman wrote it all down and she was free to go.

As she walked to her car someone in the distance was playing The Reflex by Duran Duran.

I awake, mind-numbed and exhausted as usual, the bouncing tempo of a Charleston fading from my mind – where had that come from? At first I think I am standing on pavement or road, not on a train for a change. A clanking becomes a rumble accompanied by a roar and crackle. As a faint whiff of ozone hits my senses, the rumble crescendos. I take my eyes from the ground as, inches from my face, the thunder from the tunnel to my right erupts into a red and cream blur.

Jumping back I gaze at the train as it shudders to a halt.

Back in – no, under – London again, I groan. The attire of the crowds suggests late nineteen-twenties or early thirties, evidence backed up by the adverts that adorn muted cream and green walls. Bulbs that are too dim to adequately illuminate this man-made cavern hang from the roof. The train disgorges a proportion of its passengers, to be replaced immediately by those waiting. With a mechanical sigh, the doors close and the carriages accelerate to flee the meagre light.

"You all right, son?"

The speaker wears a middle-aged face, frowning with genuine concern. His clothes suggest he is fairly well off, and he wields an umbrella and a leather briefcase. Standing an inch or two taller than me, his eyes scan me. Maybe he cannot imagine why I am dressed the way I am.

He wants to help, but he cannot help me; I am beyond help. So I ignore him and stare back at the curved wall opposite until I hear his footsteps retreat.

I try to prevent my mind thinking of a song. Curse all songs. Dangerous: they take me here, and there, and all the everywheres I have never wanted to go. I ache to stay in one place for more than a few minutes, more than a few hours – or, if that is no longer possible, to be nowhere forever.

Staring at the electrified tracks before me, I consider a way out of this mess. A permanent way. Somewhere in the twisting tunnels another rumble grows. Without further thought I step forward and over the edge. A cry from along the platform comes too late as I make sizzling contact, and I welcome the pain of electricity as it surges through me. But it conjures a dangerous song: OMD – why them again? As I begin to burn, their song, Electricity, fills my mind, and the burning stops.

I succumb to temporary painless oblivion as I transition, healed once more, to another time, another place.

Wayne screamed again and was restrained.

"I beheld the living Christ," he shouted as the orderlies tied him down.

"Yeah, Wayne," one said, "sure you did."

"He was real. He still had part of the cross nailed to his hand. I saw it with my own eyes."

They secured Wayne to the trolley and wheeled him away.

"He appeared to me on the subway," he whimpered, straining against the straps. "He did. He did."

Medication was administered by hypodermic.

I've known for a while that I can carry items with me such as clothes and food. So I try an experiment. I grip hard onto a tree and hum a song. It conjures up a place and time, another railway station – why this connection with railways? – and I go, but I materialise gripping nothing but air. So, in another place, I tie myself to an armchair and hum a tune, and the chair comes too. I leave it blocking the small carriage compartment, too large to be easily removed. Possibly a guard, perplexed by the impossibility of how it had got there, will chop it into pieces in order to clear it from the train.

Weeks later, or years earlier perhaps, I down several shots of whisky and let them work their effect upon me. Then, armed with a nail gun stolen from a hardware store, I attach my other hand to the wood of a large crate. The pain is amazing, excruciating, and I grit my teeth as I hum. There is a wrenching of wood and more pain, and part of the crate accompanies me. After scaring a man with my sudden appearance in an otherwise deserted subway carriage, I rip the nails from my flesh and hum again. In the next place, on a narrow-gauge mountain railway where people babble some kind of French at my sudden appearance, my wounds are, as usual, instantly healed.

I try again, this time securing myself to a tree with another nail gun. I hum a tune through gritted teeth but go nowhere; the pain is too intense and I rip my flesh from the tree. Now I scream out the song and it whisks me away to heal.

Cursing loudly, I realise I need a sudden death, one that prevents accidental escape.

Harry, squinting close to the computer screen, played the video clip once more. In silence it depicted the grainy view taken from a pedestrian bridge over the platforms of London's Paddington station. People in their old black and white world jerkily alight from carriages. Crisply attired, bowler-hatted businessmen march to their places of work in the capital, their seats on the train taken by holidaymakers seeking escape from that same city.

In the late nineteen-forties a railway enthusiast had filmed the scene for his own enjoyment. Six decades later, after a degree of electronic restoration, his work had been deemed worth presenting to a wider audience on DVD. But, for a change, it was not the trains that occupied Harry's attention, it was the character standing unmoving next to a trolley packed with suitcases. He was out of place, his clothes anachronistic. Despite the density of the crowds, people obviously sensed his wrongness and gave him a wide berth.

And suddenly, he was gone. Harry hit pause and shuffled back a few frames and then forwards again. In one frame the man was there, in the next he was not, and Harry hunted in vain for evidence of him walking away. The film itself didn't appear to be missing any frames as the movements of the other people were continuous. In addition, it was obvious from their reactions that some of those in the crowd had also witnessed the disappearance.

Harry showed his discovery to others, one of whom took it further. For a short while, it became news and then, just as quickly, forgotten.

But Jenny, alone and with a failed childless marriage behind her, saw it and could not forget. She obtained a copy of the DVD so she could watch Stephen disappear over and over again.

I steal a gun from an old soldier – Home Guard, I presume. The area appears war-damaged – possibly early nineteen-forties? I place the end of the barrel in my mouth, aim upwards and fire. There's no way I can survive this sudden death.

Surely…

But the hint of a song escapes from my brain as my skull is mutilated, and I am whipped away to somewhere new.

New and renewed.

Damn it.

Delicately, Martin removed pieces of cement. It was taking days as it had not been known exactly where the man's limbs were located within the block. Martin had been instructed to do as little damage to the body as possible.

The corpse and his enclosure had been carefully toppled so that the man now lay on his back, his head supported by a cushion so that the neck did not snap.

Martin discovered there were ropes embedded in the cement, tied about the body.

As he chipped away towards his goal, the radio played Love Grows, the Edison Lighthouse hit from a few months previously.

My watch tells me it is February – it lies.

But I have found a dependable song. The one song that is safe – all others are unpredictable. This one always brings me back to the same place and almost the same time.

The place is deserted and probably has been for at least a year. Long ago, the brick arches here were made into places of work or storage by enclosing both ends and installing lights and sanitation. All are now empty. Above my head, on top of the viaduct, the trains rumble along almost constantly.

So often do I come here that I always meet myself – past and future versions of 'me' all lumped together in one place and time. I know that I am, have been and will be all of them. Talking to myself is unnerving, so all of me work together on some sort of plan – the later versions of me appear to know what this plan is. I just help where I can but, on these initial visits, I am usually whisked away by a musical thought before I see the end result of the plan.

Jenny spent her retirement accumulating stories from around the world; it was amazing the things people would record on the Internet.

Always he was associated with trains and stations, and her mind constantly popped back to that last moment on the phone, and what had been playing in the background. She pondered putting the stories together and self-publishing them in a single book. But what was the point? It wouldn't bring Stephen back.

In near darkness, Vera Lynn's voice fading from my thoughts, I follow stragglers as they exit the station. Far in the distance, anti-aircraft fire arcs up into the sky as the droning comes closer, now almost overhead. Shadows of buildings surround the station; I can make out houses framed in blackness against the stars.

Shouts and screams are barely audible as German bombs begin to fall. Spurred into action, I run towards an alleyway but halt whilst still in the middle of a road, watching as a punctuated line of destruction booms closer. No longer trembling, I dare them to gift me with an instantaneous end. But the droning passes overhead leaving me unscathed.

I wander on, cursing.

After some minutes I come to a makeshift hospital; a tent erected in a park. On a whim I pick up and don an abandoned white coat while others, too engrossed in the chaos to take notice, rush to and fro in their own organised panic. There are occupied beds here – hardly beds, merely blankets on the ground – and I stand over a shivering, bloodied man who begs me to ease the pain from his shattered legs – and the plan enters my head. I now know how this can end.

A nurse enters and sees me. I shout for her to bring morphine, which she does unquestioningly. More bombs drop while I hold the bottle and a syringe. The injured man lapses into unconsciousness and the nurse stares wide-eyed as I hum the song.

Martin continued chipping away at the block. He had exposed much of the man's front and was working on freeing the left hand and arm. The strap of a wristwatch could already be made out underneath the remains of the shirt cuff. More cement was removed allowing the fabric to be pulled to one side.

He frowned over the timepiece. Its face was hidden under a thin layer of cement dust, but he could make out buttons, one on the left side, two on the right. None of them resembled a winder. Dampening a cloth he wiped the face of the watch clean and stared in amazement. Instead of hands the device sported pulsating black numbers on a yellowish-grey background. Smaller numbers constantly counted off the seconds. He had never seen anything like it.

While he stared, the Beatles sung Let It Be on the transistor radio.

With renewed purpose I gather my resources: money I steal where I can, dipping hands into tills before humming that old Bud Flanagan song. Why it should deposit me nearly forty years after its creation I put down to a childhood memory centred on the mid-nineteen-sixties. I remember that, while accompanying my father who was purchasing some furniture, we had visited a place such as this – I had stood mesmerised while passenger and goods trains thundered overhead.

Any time I discover myself near a hospital I attempt to steal morphine and syringes. These I store on a shelf underneath the arch. Below the shelf stand more than ten large bags of cement. The cement has been bought cash-on-delivery with the stolen money. In the middle of the room is the wooden box I have constructed. It stands just over five feet in height and just under three on each side.

Upon returning home Geoffrey, as usual, checked the answer phone – it held a single message. He rewound the tape and listened.

"Jenny, are you there? It's Stephen," came the muffled voice. In the background Geoffrey could hear sounds that suggested the caller was at a railway station. He raised his eyebrows and rewound the tape again without listening to the rest. Obviously a wrong number but, as far as he knew, no one called Jenny had ever occupied this flat. He had been the owner for nearly twelve years but, having just put the place on the market, that was about to change.

Three weeks later something nagged at the back of his mind while he was showing a girl called Jennifer around the place. Later, he accepted her offer to buy.

We are ready. I know it must be so as more later versions of me turn up and we all start mixing the cement. This is the first time I've managed to stay nearly to the end.

After a while one of me shouts, "It's time." We arm ourselves with the syringes and plunge them into his arms. He slumps but does not completely lose consciousness as we load him into the box. Ropes bind him in an upright position as cement is poured all about him. He smiles and drifts into sleep but does not disappear as I had feared.

I return time and time again to be the other incarnations of myself and perform the cement mixing and morphine injecting. Finally, there is only one left who I've never been – the future me held solid in the cement. The next time I return it will be me in the box. I will be at peace. On the back of an invoice for the cement I scribble a farewell note hesitating to mention Jenny's name as, at this time, she would have still been a child.

Jenny sat in the chair staring out through the windows of the home. About her, the other residents either did likewise, played cards or watched TV.

"Stephen, why didn't you come back?" she murmured, fingering the ring dangling from a chain around her neck. Her hand encountered the skin under her chin. It felt thin and loose.

"Where did my life go?" she thought.

The injections hurt for a moment but a fogginess overcomes me and I drift, thankfully without song, into a deep darkness.

"Goodbye, Jenny," is my last thought.

The hour was late but Martin was too intrigued to halt. What other treasures would he find? The wristwatch, still attached to the corpse's wrist, silently ticked off the minutes and hours. Martin had concluded that it told neither the right time nor the correct date.

One piece of cement was still locked about the legs and, once removed, the man could be lifted from his prison. Using his drills and cutting wheels Martin freed that final block, prising it up as gently as he could, making sure that he dislodged as little of the tattered clothing as possible. Ascertaining that no further damage would be done, he lifted it clear, placing it with the rest. He inspected the fully exposed man knowing his part in this was now over. Those responsible for carrying out the autopsy would be arriving in the morning.

On the radio the DJ started playing the Move's new single and Martin, being a fan, walked over to the set and turned it up, its tinny, tiny speaker distorting the sound.

Then he turned back to the corpse and became aware of something very wrong. The body was no longer static; instead, it pulsated and squirmed, and within ten beats of Martin's accelerating heart, the dry flesh had filled out.

The eyes snapped open and, seeing Martin, locked onto his own.

"Nooo, not again," the former corpse screamed as it faded from view.

Martin stared, mouth unconsciously open, at the now empty depression in the cement, but all he could remember was the expression of horror those eyes had held.

On the radio the Move played Brontosaurus.

The idea of using music as a basis for accidental time travel is not one I had come across before writing **Underneath The Arches** *in 2006. Of course, you might be of a different opinion and can point me to several. If you're not sure of when each part of this story is set – especially the sections featuring Jenny and Martin – then finding out when each of the songs mentioned appeared in the UK charts will give you some idea of the intended date.*

The Unreality Onion

Agent Pete Hampshire ducked instinctively. A whistle of bullets filled the air. He grimaced and corrected his stance. Then fired at the, as yet unknown, enemy. Beside him, Agent Carl Brunswick, took longer adjusting to the situation's unreality. Soon his own beam was lined on the source of the noise.

They'd been deposited in sparse woods. Meagre light penetrating the foliage painted the trees in stripes of grey on a greyer background. The enemy had the lower ground beyond the edge of the woods – not that it should make any difference. Unlike Pete and Carl, the enemy were unreal.

Firepower erupting from behind the two agents criss-crossed the enemy's own and, from ahead, came a torrent of curses in, if Pete wasn't mistaken, old German. So, we have our own troops as well, he thought, before wondering where the hell this place was supposed to be. On each side he became aware of camouflaged soldiers advancing down the hill alongside him.

More unreality. He wondered which side had provided them.

The German troops, recovered from their surprise, began returning fire again. Carl's power beam cut through the less-than-solid trunks of the trees and into the enemy position. Pete's eyes fell on artillery – several vehicles including three mounted guns. They looked historical. The vehicles displayed a familiar symbol. Beyond them loomed a large, old black and white building, from which erupted more troops. A flag with the same symbol hung from a window.

Inside his mouth Pete waggled his tongue and clicked his teeth together. In response, a small holographic Heads-Up Display projection appeared in front of his right eye. Under his subtle control, his implant searched through a database of symbols until a match was detected. Got it – swastika – a symbol used the world over for various reasons including good luck, wealth and nationalistic identity. Pete dug further and found a match with German usage leading up to a global conflict – twentieth century. Well, that explained the primitive weapons. He dismissed the HUD, while thinking of Janice and the kids.

He aimed his beamer at the enemy, and sliced through guns and soldiers. Beside him, Carl and the other unreal soldiers were doing the same.

Damn, he suddenly remembered that Janice's mother, Helen, was coming over for the weekend.

A few minutes later he stood beyond the tree line and surveyed the carnage. Behind him, his unreal troops awaited his next move. Somewhere in all this there had to be a clue as to why they were here and what this was all about. Carl was examining the bodies of the slain and the remains of the sliced up vehicles.

"Found a map," Carl said, returning with some folded paper. "My implant correlates it to a location in northern Europe, mid-twentieth century; a country known then as Poland."

Pete's implant scanned the map and came to the same conclusion. He nodded and looked at the troops and then at their surroundings. The air of unreality permeated everything. Pete had difficulty holding what he saw in sharp focus. Resources must be stretched thin, he thought.

"What about that?" Pete pointed to the building.

"Headquarters, possibly," Carl surmised, sweat beading his brow. Pete frowned. Carl, nearly ten years older than Pete's twenty-nine, was letting the unreality get to him – never a good sign. Time he retired – but agents were thin on the ground.

"Okay, we take a look," Pete said and nodded at the troops. He set off at a brisk pace towards the supposed headquarters. As he ran he cursed himself for agreeing to Helen's visit. He and Helen didn't get on, at least not since her husband Jacques had got himself killed in the Crusades. Damned fool was way too old to still be in service.

Nearing the building their troops were met by a sporadic burst of machine gun fire. A bullet passed harmlessly straight through Pete's torso. Carl ducked unnecessarily and responded with a beam that sliced through wood and cement. Pete rushed the door, burning down three Germans who didn't get out of his way in time – once, he might have felt something for these victims, these play figurines – but they had no life of their own.

A large hallway with an impressively decorated wide staircase led up to a panelled corridor. All doors, except the large one at the end, stood open.

Pete nodded his head towards the target.

"In there, you reckon?" Carl asked, needlessly. Pete's implant noted the quaver in Carl's voice – nervous.

Together they disintegrated the door and burst in. A single shot from the right cut across Carl's forehead. Carl swore, doing his best to disbelieve the injury. While he cut the German officer down with a beam, Pete's implant catalogued the red slash across his colleague's brow. Carl grunted and brought himself back into reality; the mark faded but was still visible.

Pete scanned the room: walls of filled bookcases; a large wooden desk; the symbol on a red, white and black flag hanging over the ornate, unlit fireplace. The clue, he felt, had to be here. He kept scanning: brass lamps, padded chairs, a coat stand, heavy curtains. The implant imaged and processed everything. On the desk were papers and a metal bust of a man's head, under the chin was a representation of that symbol again. Pete glanced at the papers, the HUD streamed into life, translating the language before his eyes – they were just orders and details of troop movements. No, they were not it. He examined the bust again, at the moustached face that stared sightlessly ahead. There was something wrong.

And then Pete got it.

The symbol had five arms instead of the four displayed elsewhere.

Pete grinned. "Gotcha."

Carl, dabbing at his forehead, joined him beside the desk.

Pete picked up the bust and examined it. The underside contained a script that flowed as his eyes tried and failed to interpret it. Sometimes it resembled a language with which he was familiar, then it would change to something symbolic like Chinese. Finally, it stabilised into a pattern which Pete's implant recorded for later analysis.

"Here we go," he heard Carl say as the room faded.

"Agent Hampshire?"

Pete's eyes cleared as his visor was removed and a familiar world returned. He was lying on a bed surrounded by the unreality synchroniser machines. A medic disconnected the sensors from his head and arms.

Colonel Staunton sat at the end of the bed. "Usual stuff?" he asked.

"Another historical sequence, sir," Pete said, pulling himself up. "No purpose as far as I could see, just went in and found the clue. German, twentieth century global war. Um…" – Pete waited for his implant to supply the information – it did – "Nazis, Hitler. The clue was a bust with an incorrect symbol – a swastika. The swirling message appeared again. Any idea what it is? What they're planning?"

"Oh, intelligence is full of the usual crap. All we know is that the clues are becoming less coherent, no one can identify a pattern to either the messages or the locations." Staunton put a hand on Agent Hampshire's shoulder. "We lost Barton. Not sure what happened – we're trying to recover the data from his implant. Think he was on to something, though. Came back through repeating nothing but 'too deep' over and over until he died."

"Jesus. Barton was the best. Taught me everything I…"

Another pat on the shoulder.

"Yes, I know. How's Carl holding up?"

Pete sighed.

"Thought so. Didn't need to see that scar on his head to know it's getting to him."

"When's the next mission?" Pete asked.

"You're free for a week at least – use it wisely."

"Pah. Not with Helen over."

But the next few days were, initially, a relief. Helen seemed to have mellowed in her distrust of Pete and his work. Whether this was for his sake or for Janice's, he wasn't sure. Helen seemed to blame him personally for her loss, just because he and Jacques had both worked for the same organisation. Or maybe Helen blamed him for marrying her daughter, for putting Janice though the same torment Jacques had put her through. Pete had given up trying to analyse it. His implant nagged that it could try to figure out the change in Helen's stance – Pete quietened it with a tongue gesture and a sharp click of his molar. But his mind wouldn't let it go.

On the final afternoon of Helen's visit, the three sat chatting out in the small communal garden, shared with nearby neighbours. Robert and Alice played in the bushes.

"So, Pete. Are we winning?" Helen asked, suddenly changing the topic from gardening.

Oh, here it comes, Pete thought.

"I thought you agreed not to talk about it, Mum," Janice scolded.

"Oh, I miss the news – you know… the real inside news. The stuff they put out for the public says nothing."

Pete watched the children play tag around the garden. He didn't want to talk about it. Sitting here, in the warmth of a spring sun, he tried to forget about his other life.

"Well, Pete?" Helen insisted. Pete took a deep breath. Janice exhaled in a meaningful manner.

"The tactics are changing but we don't know what they're leading up to, if anything. Maybe they're running out of ideas. They're certainly not gaining any ground."

"But are we? Jacques used to tell me that we were winning, slowly. But it's been going on for so many years now that I just can't remember what we've won or lost."

"Mum, leave it."

"Yes, but I want to know," Helen retorted, leaning forwards in her chair, wagging a finger at her daughter. "Is it really all worth it in the end? Just what are we fighting for anyway? What's the advantage of having all this so-called unreality?"

Pete grunted, got up and went inside the house. Fixing himself a drink, he could still hear Janice outside, having words with her mother.

The doorbell rang and Pete found Carl standing on his doorstep. The mark across his forehead was still quite prominent. Red. Pete thought, I bet they've…

"They've transferred me," Carl confirmed, his hands shaking.

"Ah, sorry, Carl. Come in. Helen's here – you remember Jacques?"

"Oh yes, of course. Sorry," Carl whispered, his eyes darting around, a worried expression flitting across his features. "I didn't mean to intrude."

"No problem – drink?" Carl nodded. "Join us out in the garden."

Outside, Pete re-introduced Carl and Helen, who immediately started her questioning on Carl.

"Mum," Janice chided, but Helen persisted.

Pete watched the children in a dreamy fashion while letting the conversation pass him by, glad to no longer be the subject of Helen's interrogation. He thought about how alike the kids were – despite the eighteen-month difference. Robert was nearly as tall as his sister, and had the same body shape and mannerisms. Dressed similarly, he found he almost had trouble telling them apart as they chased each other. He shook his head and stared at them more attentively. There was an almost ethereal presence as they laughed and flowed in and out of the bushes.

Too much sun, Pete thought as he poured the rest of the cool drink down his throat.

Carl and Helen were still talking about unreality – Pete thought Carl would fend the older woman off gracefully but, listening in, he realised that the subject had veered towards things that Carl should not have been commenting upon. He put it down to Carl's change of circumstances and wondered, should I caution him? Subtly? He is my colleague.

When Carl started talking about the mission with the Germans, Pete sat up about to interject but he stopped, staring at the scar on Carl's forehead.

Something was wrong.

Hadn't the bullet grazed the skin over his right eye?

"Carl," he said, reaching out a hand to the scar. "Hold still a moment."

As Pete's hand connected to the clue, swirling text including the words 'too deep' writhed across Carl's face before the sun went out.

"Carl?" Pete shouted, waking up on the bed surrounded, as usual, by the unreality machines. He pulled the sensors off his arm. "Janice?"

A man who, without close inspection, could have been mistaken for Colonel Staunton came into the room.

"Ah, Agent Hampton. Peter."

Something inside Pete jarred – he couldn't identify what.

"You're back with us again."

"I, uh, did I just, um…"

"Yes, I know. Damned stuff gets us believing anything, doesn't it?"

"Janice?"

"Janet."

"Oh, yes."

"Home with your daughter. You're due for a few days leave."

"Daughter. Oh… Carl. Agent Brunswick."

"Unreal."

"Shit."

"Sorry, nasty trick to play on you. Seems like they believed it, though. How's your mother-in-law?"

"What?"

"Fading fast, is it? Just as well. Carl was a trap for her and they fell for it."

"Helen? What's she got to do with this?"

"Nothing – not the real one anyway."

"Oh yes, I see. Helen. Hell."

Pete sat with Janet in the garden watching Alice making a daisy chain on the small lawn.

"What's wrong?" Janet asked. "You've been staring at Alice as if you can't believe she's there."

"Nothing really – oh, work – the unreality. There was a set-up – they made me believe other things…"

"What? That Alice had died?" Janet said, her voice reduced to a whisper. "The bastards."

"No, not that. But Alice had… had a brother."

"Robert," she whispered, after a moment.

"Yes," Pete gulped. He agreed – they were bastards. Robert had died soon after birth, about when Alice was eighteen months old. Alice didn't remember – one day they'd have to tell her that she'd once had a brother. *The bastards made Robert part of the unreality they wove around me.* Pete tried to console himself – at least they'd caught one of the enemy, so it had all been worthwhile.

Hadn't it?

Hell, he was feeling like Carl.

Damn. He had to remind himself that Carl hadn't existed, either.

Twenty-nine, he thought. I can apply for retirement from active duty after next birthday.

Alice finished weaving her chain of flowers and brought them for inspection. Pete watched. The chain was perfect – each flower identical and threaded to the next in exactly the same style – he had a sinking feeling.

"They're lovely, darling," Janet crooned.

No, they're not, Pete realised. He glanced around the garden, at the small suburban houses, at the fluffy clouds in the blue sky, at the green leaves on the trees.

Perfect.

Perfectly unreal.

Everything started to lose focus.

He reached out and touched the ring of flowers, which shimmered, petals turning into symbols, into words.

"Pete?" Janet said. "Peter."

"Daddy."

God. How deep does this go?

Outside the glass tank, the smaller of the two grey creatures turned to the other.

"It's breaking through another level," it would have said, had it possessed a mouth. It said it anyway, in its own fashion.

The other creature analysed the settings on the machines. Inside the glass tank, the misshapen torso quivered slightly. However, the thousands of micro-fine wire connections linking the body to the machines prevented too much movement.

The larger creature felt pity. What would the poor thing feel when it broke through the final level of unreality? Did it understand the messages they were trying to send it? Would the truth drive it completely insane? Should they put it out of its misery now?

The creature observed the face, or at least as much of the face as could be seen. Bunches of wires entered the skull where there should have been eyes, mouth and ears. Tubes provided nourishment and oxygen. Wires attached to the stumps of arms and legs provided sensations as if such limbs were still possessed. But the body, ancient and shrivelled, and the last of its kind, was barely alive.

"If only we had arrived a century or so ago, we might have saved them," the smaller creature trilled.

"Or maybe not. Don't blame yourself, love." The larger creature extended a pseudopod-like projection to its mate. Chemicals of comfort were exchanged. "They did this to themselves. We are merely witnessing the end."

"But they did it to save themselves, dear. Before their world completely died."

"The machines are a work of genius, though."

"Yes, it's a pity we couldn't determine their function earlier."

"They scare me."

"I also. They seem to exist independently, propagating through the dimensions of unreality that they create."

"They do exist fully here, though. Don't they?"

And somewhere far away, yet close enough to be almost overlapping, a tear fell from an observer's eye.

The Unreality Onion *also appears in the* 2021 SciFi Anthology: The Science Fiction Novelists *edited by E J Runyon and Katherine Kirk (ISBN: 9798701281538) along with two more of my science fiction stories. You can find it here:*

   https://www.amazon.co.uk/dp/B08V5LXLKQ/

Fair Exchange

"A timeslip?"

"Yes."

"What? You mean where you imagine you go back into the past and see actual events and things?"

"Yes, but I didn't imagine it."

"Oh yeah? And how do you know you didn't?"

"Simple. Look at this book."

"Did you write this?"

"Don't be silly, that's not my handwriting. No, I was, er… given it by someone… from back then."

"Given it? That's impossible. Surely, timeslips, from the little I've heard, are just supposed to let you view the past, not to interact with it."

"That's what I thought, but apparently not in my case. Anyway, he didn't exactly give the book to me; I was just holding it when I returned back here. You don't have much control over timeslips, you know."

"Really…"

"Well, anyway, this book is his diary. And I, um, left him with something of mine in exchange."

"Oh yeah, what?"

"Couple of things actually."

"Well?"

"My tablet."

"What, your new Android?"

"Yeah, that's right."

"And the second thing?"

"I'd just plugged in the solar powered charger when I timeslipped."

"So, you lost that as well?"

34

"It wasn't deliberate. I was holding his diary – he had hold of my tablet. Probably a fair exchange when you think about it."

"Yeah, right… So just how far back into the past am I to believe you travelled?"

"Er… well, I reckon I must have gone right back to, um… fifteen, twenty-four or so."

"Fifteen…"

"…twenty-four."

"And you expect me to believe that? Even if it was true, don't you realise the consequences of leaving such a modern device in the past? You could have changed the entire course of history."

"Well, that's the interesting part… I think what I actually did was to make sure that something happened back then that wouldn't have happened had I not timeslipped."

"Oh, and what, pray, would that have been?"

"Well, this guy I met, he was in a bit of a state at the time, as you will see if you read the diary. He'd just graduated from university; studied medicine, such as it was at the time. And he was trying to help with that plague trouble that they were having back then."

"What, you mean the Black death?"

"Yeah. Anyway, I showed him a medical app I'd downloaded."

"You always were a hypochondriac."

"Thanks a lot. Well, anyway, I found some info on the plague… and how to cure it."

"And he understood what the tablet was telling him?"

"Oh yes, after a short while, only a few minutes in fact, he became quite proficient in its use. Well, tablets are not exactly rocket science, are they? Young kids can use them. And he was rather bright."

"And…?"

"Well, I, er, gather he went off and cured lots of people; hundreds, possibly more. Became quite well known for it, in fact."

"So, you are saying that, because you had this timeslip, thousands of people were saved from dying of the plague back in fifteen, uh…"

"…twenty-four. Yes."

"And this is well documented in the history books, is it?"

"Actually, it wasn't really the plague problem that he was mostly famous for."

"Oh yes… please continue…"

"Well, I'd also installed a history app – it covered all the major events from the dawn of civilisation right up to the present."

"Ah, and how did he make use of that, then?"

"Well, he, um… actually, I suppose I ought to tell you his name."

"Umm?"

"He was called Michel…"

"Michel. Michel what?"

"…de Nostredame."

"Who?"

"Nostradamus."

"Oh."

Fair Exchange *was an exercise in writing a story that consisted only of dialogue. It deliberately doesn't even mention the names of the characters speaking the words. The original version of the story was written in 2000 so, for this collection, it was updated to use more modern technology.*

The Wrong Parth

Is it right to be scared of my stomach?

I stare down at it, at the bulge, at the impossibility of the life that grows inside.

It shouldn't be there. I hate it.

"Who was he? Where did you find him?" the other girls ask, incredulous. "Where is he now?"

Well, that's what they asked three months ago when the condition became apparent.

I had no answers then.

I still have no answers.

That's not quite true. In my pocket I have one answer. They don't know I have it.

Ever since my condition became known I have been kept at the hospital – a prisoner in all but name. Most of them want to smother me in protection to ensure that no harm comes to what I carry. Others want to take me apart, to see exactly what lurks inside me. They did scans, it looks normal. Female, without a doubt.

But doubt, they still do.

And I have no idea how it got there.

I am forty-one. There are not many that are younger than me. Maybe there are some who are as young as thirty-eight. I am forty-one – the only pregnant woman in the world. Of the two billion of us left, why am I the only one burdened to carry a new life?

I didn't ask for this.

I was two years old when all the men died. I read about it in school, back when there were still girls young enough to require schooling. I don't remember men. I have no memories of ever having met one. Not even my father. Yes, I know we can watch them in the old videos and TV programmes. But I have never known men in my life and, no, I have never known a man, either, in that other sense of the word.

But that doesn't stop the thing that shouldn't be inside me from being there, and it's getting bigger every day.

Some of them want to take samples to see if they can identify who or what the father could possibly be. Others are scared that any intrusion could damage it. That doesn't worry me. I don't care about what's inside me, not in any positive way, at least – I have never been taught to care about such things. The teachers no longer had any reason to trouble us with such caring. They merely taught all of us growing up in this diminishing world to understand and accept the eventual oblivion of our species.

I had to look up *parthenogenesis* after I'd heard it whispered a few times. Asexual reproduction. Fish, birds and reptiles have been known to do it – it doesn't happen in mammals, apparently.

My body never read the rule book.

We'd learned in school about the things that had been tried: the wholesale raiding of the old sperm banks only to discover nothing of human male origin had survived; the endless failed cloning experiments; the desperate attempts to induce artificial parthenogenesis when nothing else worked.

Nothing else ever did work.

And then my body did this. I had no say in the matter.

Some see me as a new hope, but all I see is a curse. If I am the only one then what is the point? Will I have a daughter whose fate is to be the last human? What kind of legacy is that to bequeath to someone?

I know they search the world for another like me. Even if they find a hundred, it won't be enough.

My hand clasps the box of pills in my pocket. Its presence is comforting.

They don't know I have something that will end the false hope, extinguish the curse. This is a hospital – such things can be found if one searches hard enough.

I am scared of what is in my stomach, but I am increasingly less scared of what the pills will do…

To both of us.

One of the main influences here was John Wyndham's tale Consider Her Ways, *which deals with a society consisting solely of women. In that story's case the society had already figured out the problem of procreation. In 2015, when* **The Wrong Parth** *was written, I was contemplating a society where they hadn't…*

The Paradox Engineers

A paradox in (roughly) three parts

Part 1a – Cause or Effect

1.1 – Anchors Aweigh

"Kill yer granddad," said Preston, the chief technician.

Duncan grimaced. Like that old 'Break a leg' thing actors said, it was no longer funny. He wondered if it had ever been funny. Beside him, a sneer passed across Xander's lips as he continued to check the locator strapped to his wrist. Duncan had already checked his own.

Preston secured the two of them into the module. Each seat was contoured to their bodies, preventing unnecessary movement.

Located in a niche above their heads sat their time controller – the TC. The featureless cube, small enough to hold in the hand, had no controls, no ornamentation, and no obvious way to open it. Dull grey, it gave no clue as to what its capabilities were – just the way it should be. Its capabilities, for those who knew, were around thirty years, give or take, from the point in time where it first happened to be.

Duncan tested the controller by thinking at it. It responded as expected. He felt Xander's mind caress the device as well. Though he could not read Xander's thoughts directly, the feeling was the nearest thing to telepathy ever invented, courtesy of electronics and genetics far beyond their understanding. This was their personal TC – tuned to their minds only.

While Preston sealed the door, Duncan adjusted the position of the bag strapped to his chest. Within it were a change of clothing, some water and, most importantly, his matter converter – a thin rectangular device also tuned to his mind.

"Happy landings," Preston's muffled voice called from outside as a short countdown started.

Duncan hated this part and was glad he'd only eaten a light breakfast.

Just before zero both he and Xander tensed, trying to make as little movement as possible.

1.2 – Why They Went To All The Trouble

"Something's wrong," Charles Alton said, "and we want to send you two back to see what it is and what you can do to fix it."

"Rogues?" Xander asked.

"Possibly," Alton shrugged. "We are detecting that the nineteen seventies are becoming unstable. They were fine a few weeks ago. But now history is being eroded. A number of people are registering as dead when they shouldn't be and vice versa."

"Ancient history," Xander said. No one had been back as far as the twentieth century as yet.

"Anyone famous?" Duncan asked.

"Not really. At the moment mainly just a couple of politicians, and a minor music celebrity. Probably several others whose history was never recorded."

"So, do we need to go back and kill them, or make sure they stay alive?" Xander said.

Alton sighed. "Well, that's the problem. We're not sure. There's conflicting information as to exactly what their influence was. So, at the moment, we're not certain which timeline is the one that irrevocably leads back to here."

"So, if we find a rogue killing one of them then we need to stop them," Duncan said.

"And kill the rogue if he's trying to keep them alive," Xander added. "Not exactly cut and dry, is it?"

Alton shrugged again, a familiar habit recently. The rogue time travellers, whoever they were, seemed intent on screwing up history.

"Here's a list of those we've managed to pin down. We hope to have a few others by the time you are ready to leave."

Duncan scanned the list. None of the names meant anything to him.

1.3a – How It Didn't Happen

Outside the module, Preston pressed a button and a howl reverberated around the room. Inside the module, the gut-wrenching started and the contents of the module were catapulted over six hundred years into the past to land in 1970 or thereabouts.

Once the noise had died down Preston would open the door to make sure it was as empty as expected. The two seats would be devoid of their occupants as would be the niche between them. Also, and most importantly, there would be no blood. Then, as usual, he would breathe a sigh of relief, shut down all the electronics and head to the cafeteria for a coffee.

Well, that was what should have happened.

Only, it didn't.

Part 2 – The Effect

2.1 – Boiled Insurance Agent

"What, again?" said Johnny Cliché. "I'm sick of boiled insurance agent."

"Well, leave it then," said his mother, Alison, heaving her rotund body around the table.

Johnny prodded the remains of the Man from the Pru and then pushed the plate aside, saying, "Don't want it."

"Don't you come crying to me later on saying you're starving," Alison scolded, snatching the plate away.

In the kitchen, she muttered, "Don't know why I bother," as she disposed of the left over meat, spinach husks and blackened potatoes.

At least Matilda, the Vietnamese pot-bellied pig, wasn't fussy and tucked into the meat and gristle with vigour. Alison looked in the fridge hoping the irregular power cuts wouldn't spoil the meat too soon – there was still plenty of him left. At least he'd been tastier than the Avon lady – proper protein was becoming hard to come by. It was mainly provided by a few simple souls who insisted on carrying on as if things were still normal. Johnny and Alison usually managed to relieve them of that delusion.

Slumped in the lounge, Johnny sulked while his mother clattered dirty plates and cutlery through the washing up water. He sat nursing his hunger whilst watching TV. It was showing lizards being pecked to death by budgerigars. Johnny was bored by it – he'd seen it before. He flicked through the channels but there wasn't much else on: BBC2 was showing a stomach operation and ITV was broadcasting a game show where naked contestants were being given electric shocks when they got an answer wrong. One guy was having his genitals fried off – the audience howled with laughter.

Johnny sighed, surely it hadn't always been like this, had it? He wanted to return to the future when Channels 4 and 5 started up or even later when digital arrived. But his dad had managed to ground him yet again.

2.2 – Sweet Dreams

"Time for bed," Johnny's mum said. It was half-past nine.

He complained with his usual, "It's too early, I'm nearly eight," excuse but Alison wasn't having any of it, so he shrugged and trudged up the stairs. Anyway, he was nearly only eight because, at that moment, it was late 1976. He didn't feel nearly eight – sometimes he felt like he was ninety-eight.

On the landing a spider was spinning a web in between the wooden banister rails. For a few seconds he watched it delicately connect the strands together. Then he killed it. He contemplated eating it but flicked it down the stairs instead. It was probably too small even for Matilda's permanent appetite to find.

He thought about running away again but the London Underground strike was in its fifth year and buses were even rarer than insurance agents.

In bed he tried to fast forward to when he was twenty-one. By then he would be having wonderful sex with Natalie before she went off to fight and die in the nuclear devastation that had been or will be the Gulf War. He tried to imagine her full, voluptuous form but his nearly eight-year-old body wouldn't respond as he knew it had done when he had been older.

He sighed. His dad had buggered things up again. Maybe it was some new sort of anti-time-travel force field. So Johnny was stuck in the latter half of the nineteen seventies. All he managed to do was to mess up a few minor timelines.

As he tried to get to sleep he could hear the sounds of this depressing decade leaking into the house from the days and years crowding nearby: punk rock bands down the street trying their best not to learn too many guitar chords; workers on strike during the Winter of Complete Bloody Chaos; simultaneously, but later on, those same workers tearing down the Houses of Parliament after executing prime minister Jim Callaghan; Pong machines bleeping in pubs; the ominous Jaws shark music. The last thing he heard before dropping off was Marc Bolan's car crashing into a tree at two hundred miles an hour.

Sweet dreams.

2.3 – DIY Breakfast

Some years later or maybe earlier, Johnny was no longer sure, he awoke almost before the sun rose. His stomach rumbled – he couldn't remember if he'd eaten the day before or not. He couldn't even recall how old he'd been or which year it had been the previous day. He cursed his dad and crept downstairs to sneak a peek in the fridge.

As he entered the kitchen two squirrels dashed out the pig-flap. He managed to kick a third up the arse before it escaped. Pity he hadn't been quieter coming down – grilled squirrel was one of his favourites but they were a bastard to catch. Even Matilda, currently asleep in her basket, wasn't fast enough.

The fridge held little to tempt him. There was a plate of meat – he wasn't sure if it was Man from the Pru, Avon lady or Jehovah's Witness. Either way, it was ancient and completely unappetising. Even the milk was used up – the empty bottle sat there, the thin white scum on the bottom mocking him. He had a thought and went to the front door to see if the rare daily delivery had turned up. He was in luck for a change – amongst the broken glass stood a single shiny bottle. At least the milkmen were still providing service of a kind, though it was often combined with bringing the post and any number of less legal black market operations. Having seen the gleam in his eye more than once, his mother had to remind him that milkmen were off limits.

He inspected the foil lid – it already showed signs of attack. He left the bottle where it was and crept back against the stairs, leaving the door wide open. Unmoving, he waited fifteen minutes before the blue tit plucked up the courage to return. The stone from Johnny's catapult hit the bird square in the eye and it flopped down dead or unconscious, he didn't care which, on the front doorstep.

"Snap, crackle, pop," Johnny muttered a short time later before forcing the de-feathered remains of the dead bird into his mouth. His teeth splintered the bones which did go snap, crackle and pop. The residue of milk in the breakfast bowl was tainted a delicate shade of pink.

Johnny licked his lips, and swilled the plate and spoon clean under the kitchen tap before returning to bed.

2.4 – Back and Forth

Johnny sensed his dad was near. The elusive git was probably watching him from a few minutes in the future or past. One day he'd catch the old fool and dismantle his time disruptor thingy once and for all.

He tried to remember the future to determine whether or not he would ever catch his father, but he couldn't recall. Not that it meant anything – remembering the future was a bugger of a thing to do – especially when it kept changing. And it did seem to be changing more than ever just recently. And so did the past. At the moment it felt like 1975 but his body disagreed – it appeared to be aged around nine or ten, so it was probably later.

Time was like that.

And time was his dad's domain.

He imagined his dad in a Darth Vader helmet sucking air in and out as he talked. He wasn't like that, of course, but Johnny often wished he was – he'd prefer that to the boring reality.

He cursed his dad again and moved his mind onto a more pleasurable subject – Natalie. The later the year, the closer he was to meeting her again. In most cases they were both fourteen when they first met, though once she'd been older than him and a couple of times he'd been way older than her. Maybe this time he'd figure out how to prevent her getting called up for military service. He sighed. She was – will be – a damned good shag. At least he could still remember her. He'd drawn a reasonable facsimile of her face and body in the notebook he kept hidden under the debris in his sock drawer. In order to prevent himself from forgetting her he looked at it at least three times a week, and even more when the weeks were longer.

He went outside and leant against the silver birch tree that dominated the bottom of what they laughingly referred to as the garden. He tried to be as nonchalant as possible as he scanned the rest of the tangle of overgrown plants and discarded junk.

Maybe his dad would make a mistake and reveal himself, but the wily old sod didn't put in an appearance that day.

2.5 – Unreliable Memories

"I hate stewed dandelions – you know that," Johnny shouted, tipping the plate over onto the table. "Why can't we catch some dogs or cats? This shit tastes like shit."

"Don't swear," his mother scolded, scraping the remains off the table and into Matilda's food bowl. "One more tantrum like that and I'll get your dad to give you a good hiding."

"Yeah, like that old sod ever comes round any more. It's a wonder he ever managed to fuck you pregnant in the first place."

"Young man. You will go and wash your mouth out with soap and bleach this instant. Bathroom. Now – GO."

Johnny smirked to himself while Alison propelled him through the house by the scruff of his shirt collar. It wasn't often he managed to make her lose her temper and, after all these years, it was satisfying to know he still could. She crammed the block of carbolic into his mouth, following it with bleach and scouring powder. She made him chew it for ten whole minutes.

"Let that be a lesson to you," she said while Johnny spat blood and skin into the sink. The bleeding stopped after a few minutes and he could feel the timelines adjusting around himself to erase the damage.

Under his breath he vowed revenge on the old bitch as soon as he was big enough. When would he ever be big enough? He was seven years old again. How many times had he been seven? More than he could count, that's what.

In his room he pulled out the drawing of Natalie. It was wrong – surely her tits used to be bigger than that? He cursed loudly and then, remembering his mother downstairs, cursed softly. His bastard father must have screwed with his memories yet again.

2.6 – Victory, Maybe?

Sneaking along the landing, Johnny kept as quiet as he could. The sound of his dad's voice came from his mother's bedroom. Trust his old man to appear in the past instead of the future.

Johnny felt the knife in the grip of his six-year-old hand and hoped it would be adequate. The blade was long and sharp enough. His small stature was the only fly in the ointment. Why hadn't this happened when he was thirteen?

"I'm doing this for you, Natalie," he thought, picturing the stick-thin figure in his drawing, knowing it to be utterly wrong but unable to remember the correct potential reality. "Hold on, girl, I'm coming to save you."

The door was slightly ajar. Good, that would be in his favour. He held the knife behind him and peered through the gap. His father's back was towards him. His mother, her eyes red, appeared too preoccupied to notice Johnny. At least, that's what he hoped. Somehow, she appeared slimmer than she had of late, more like distant memories of her that he had not seen for many years. He was sure she hadn't looked like that the last time he had been six.

He pushed the thoughts away as irrelevant and licked his lips as he contemplated his soon-to-be victory.

"What are you doing skulking around out there, Johnny?" his mother snapped.

Shit – he shouldn't have let his thoughts delay him. As his father started to turn, Johnny rushed in screaming and brandishing the knife in a manner that even he thought was a little ridiculous. He knew his dad would either swat him aside like some annoying fly, or escape into the future or past. So it came as a complete surprise when he just stood there laughing and ruffling Johnny's hair as the knife plunged into his side. But his father couldn't sustain the laugh for long – it became a gurgle as pain shot across his face. With blood pouring out of him, his legs buckled and he fell to the floor, face down.

He turned his head and looking Johnny straight in the eye, gasped, "Got you, Johnny."

With eyes still open, Johnny's father fell silent.

Johnny stared down at the corpse while his mother removed the knife, wiping it on a tissue.

"Is he really dead?" he whispered.

Alison sucked in her lips and sat down on the bed, bloodshot eyes fixed on the knife resting on her lap. He could see that she was trembling, and couldn't understand why she wasn't telling him off.

She grunted as the body faded away. Johnny was confused – had his father escaped yet again?

"Did I really kill him?" he asked, softly. Where had his father gone? He stared at his mother. Why was she even slimmer and blonder than she'd been only minutes previously? Also, why did the name Natalie keep popping into his head? He didn't know anyone called Natalie.

His hands felt as if they were shrinking. Within seconds they were like those of a baby and it was getting harder to think. As he'd done so many times before,

Johnny tried to fix things by altering the timelines.

But reality and time fought back(wards).

Part 3 – The Paradox Engineers

3.1 – How They Collected Themselves Together

Time travel wasn't an exact science. Well, the science part worked well enough, if you didn't mind the gut-wrenching travel and the fact that what was neatly assembled in the transfer module at the journey's start, wasn't anywhere quite as organised when it tumbled out at the other end. At least, the technology had advanced long past the stage where primary parts were splattered across the landscape upon arrival.

As soon as he landed, Xander mentally picked up the TC's location – it had deposited itself in London within two miles and six months of its intended location. He found it had materialised in May 1969, whilst he found himself, according to his locator, in a Welsh valley in August of the same year.

He noted how weak the TC's signal was – too distant to be usable. Still, this had been expected; it had been the longest jump ever attempted. Unexpectedly, though, his matter converter had died in the jump. He removed the rectangle from the bag, opened it up and attempted to feed it some stones and grass. But it refused to take his mental orders and a much needed cup of coffee failed to materialise.

Over the next few days he managed to find his way out of Wales and got as far as Reading by copying something called hitchhiking that he'd observed others doing. Once within thirty five miles of the country's capital, his connection with the TC was strong enough to risk jumping directly into London. He did so and greeted Duncan, who had already arrived.

"Nine bloody months," Duncan moaned.

Duncan, when he materialised, couldn't mentally locate the TC and correctly assumed he'd preceded it. He sighed – it wasn't the first time. He did have a habit of bouncing a bit further than Xander. His locator initially indicated he was somewhere to the south west of London. Then it recalculated to tell him he'd arrived on the Isle of Wight in late August 1968. He had no idea how long he would have to wait until the TC arrived. Getting around without the ability to space and time travel was going to be a bit of an inconvenience.

He tried to make himself blend in with the locals, utilising his matter converter to create suitably authentic clothing. T-shirts and torn jeans seemed to be the current fashion.

There were plenty of people about, so Duncan followed a friendly bunch who seemed to know where they were headed. As they walked he let them talk about themselves without giving much away about himself. They shared food and drink, he reciprocated by offering similar food courtesy of the matter converter hidden in his bag. If they were curious as to why his bag seemed to hold so much, they didn't comment. Indeed, most of them had the air of sleepwalkers about them. Duncan wondered why this was.

They convened in a field amongst a few thousand others and he heard musicians playing in the distance. Much of it was awful.

3.2 – Hippy Gumbo

It was early evening and, apparently, the noise was going to continue throughout the night and into a second day. Duncan accepted an offer to stay and share a ramshackle tent with half a dozen others. They didn't, however, want to go to sleep immediately. First they made a small fire and cooked some sort of pre-prepared stew. Duncan had never before experienced such a taste – called gumbo it contained meat along with hot, spicy vegetables and was even richer than some of the curries he'd once encountered on a trip to the twenty-fourth century.

After the meal Duncan was tired but the others were more interested in lounging outside the tent to inhale the smouldering leaves of some dried plant material. Not wanting to appear rude, he followed their example. After a short period he found his head swimming strangely and the appearance of ordinary objects seemed to distort in very interesting fashions. Even the so-called music, still pumping away in the distance, became more palatable. The sound seemed to leak over into his visual cortex so that everything he focussed upon shimmered with the erratic, colourful tempo. Some people began to dance or pair off. He vaguely worried that the inhaled substances could have an adverse effects upon his enhanced genetics and brain augmentations but the substances themselves allowed him to dismiss this. After a while he found it inexplicably hilarious when the people, the music and everything around them merged into one pulsating movement. Laughing, he gave in to it – plunging deep, letting it devour him.

He became aware again some hours later as the sun began to rise. Music still rattled and thumped. Lying half out of the tent, he was embarrassed to find that he was only wearing a pair of underpants. Stretched out next to him was a completely naked female. The woman had not been part of the original party and he only had vague recollections of her from the night before. Coupled with the residue of the inhaled substances, her long blonde hair and willowy form were doing strange things to his emotions. He shook his head and located the rest of his possessions inside the tent. After dressing, and while out of sight of anyone else, he ordered the matter converter to dispense something to fix his mental state, which he swallowed immediately.

The female, whose name he discovered was Alison, seemed uninterested in finding out where her own clothes had gone. Instead, she prepared a breakfast consisting of bread and left over stew, accompanying them with strong tea brewed on a portable cooker. Duncan considered offering her some clothes manufactured by the matter converter but thought the idea that a man might be routinely carrying women's clothing around might be misconstrued.

The music was still rattling away and, after they and some of the others had eaten, Alison expressed interest in viewing the musicians at closer range before they finished. "You coming with me to see them?" she asked. Duncan declined with the excuse that his head felt tender, something that hadn't been a lie earlier on.

"Okay, see you later, then," she said and shrugged. Then she wandered off, still naked and totally unconcerned about it, towards one of the marquees where the musicians continued to make their noise.

3.3 – Exit Stage Left

When no one was looking Duncan slipped away from the tent and left the field. During the past few hours his matter converter had managed to gather enough information to enable it to reproduce the local currency. His locator had also analysed a quantity of radio chatter, which allowed it to determine a route and discover methods of transport. He decided, therefore, to head for London.

By early evening he had negotiated his way via ferry to Southampton. At the railway station he boarded a train headed for London. Once in the city he manufactured more currency, enough to pay for a small lodging near Victoria Station. There he waited for the mental signal that indicated the arrival of the TC.

It took several months during which he had ample opportunity to make himself familiar with the city.

The TC finally arrived. Duncan located it and, under the cover of darkness, retrieved it from the residential garden into which it had deposited itself. In the lodging he probed it for signs of Xander. Nothing yet, but there was something odd about his perception of the timeline around the turn of the millennium. He shrugged – he had to locate Xander first.

He went forwards in time. Thirteen weeks flew past in a few seconds and there it was, faintly, Xander's mental signature. He pushed forward another seven days to meet his companion jumping in from Reading.

"Nine bloody months," Duncan moaned.

"Hah, a week for me," Xander laughed, then serious. "Right, what have we got?"

"Dunno, but I've got a funny feeling there's something wrong about thirty years ahead. We should investigate."

3.4 – How Had It Come To This?

"You saw it too?" Duncan said, his face a shade or two lighter.

"Yeah," was all Xander offered. His face, too, betrayed the shock he was trying to conceal.

The future no longer existed.

Everything ended around 2002. Nothing left, nothing habitable anyway. Devastation in all directions. Duncan imagined melted icecaps and continents blasted clear of life. Whatever the reality was, it meant there was no way to get back home, if home still existed more than six hundred years hence.

They had both briefly travelled forward to the point things went completely wrong and the TC's automatic safeties had flung them back to 1999.

"One hell of an end of the century party," Xander said, but Duncan could hear the quaver in his voice.

Duncan grimaced. "But what went wrong? We haven't done anything. Not yet anyway."

"As far as we know," Xander sighed. "Of course, it might be the rogues. They might be this far back."

"Well, if they're here as well, they're as trapped as we are."

3.5 – First Sign Of The Rogue

"Okay, we've got to figure out whether the rogues have caused this or we've done something ourselves," Xander said.

They were in early 1979. Duncan stared out the window. Snow fell on bags of rubbish that were piling up in the street.

Then Duncan's eyes glazed and his brow furrowed. "Wait, there's an extra signature in the TC."

Xander made connection. There was definitely an anomaly. "That's yours, isn't it? Very close, anyway."

"Yes. No," Duncan said. "There are minor differences."

"It's impossible. It's locked to our minds only. Are the rogues getting that clever now?" Xander said, quietly.

"We need to trace it. Find where it's coming from, when it started, what it's doing."

They checked the readings and found three incursions. The first was in 1990, the second five years earlier and the most recent one here in 1979.

Duncan slipped back to the moment the latest one appeared, a few days before in real time, and was surprised when the TC had no objection in its acceptance of the rogue signal.

Xander joined him. Duncan ran some analysis routines on the signature which might pinpoint exactly how it had been inserted.

"Anything?" he asked.

"Local," Duncan confirmed. "No attempt to hide the source, distance or direction. Weird, it's as if whoever did this has no idea of security. Anyway, I got a fix. Follow me, though maybe not too close until we know what we're dealing with."

Xander nodded as Duncan dematerialised.

3.6 – An Unexpected Face, Or Two

The house was to the west of London, in Heston, not far from Heathrow Airport. An ascending plane droned overhead whilst, not much further away, a similar vehicle descended. Duncan examined the dwelling and sensed the rogue inside. For some reason the rogue didn't feel dangerous.

The residence was of a semi-detached construction amongst a row of others of similar build. Not the most affluent but far from the slums on the eastern side of the city. A thin layer of snow covered everything apart from the road and pavements where it was merely slush.

Xander's arrival close by, but out of sight, was made clear to him via the TC, so he moved towards the front door. On the floor of the recessed porch stood a glass bottle full of milk. Duncan noted that the foil top was punctured. He frowned – how unhygienic. There was no bell so his hand moved towards the knocker but the door swung open before his hand connected.

"Hi, Duncan," Alison said.

Duncan stared at the woman, now aged by more than ten years since their last encounter and this time, at least, wearing clothes. A cat rushed in past Duncan's legs. He noticed a dead mouse dangling from its mouth before it disappeared through a side door into a room.

"Oh, there you are, Matilda," Alison said. "Damn thing's been out all night in this weather. Well, at least she won't need any breakfast."

The sound of footsteps clumping down the stairs resulted in the appearance of a boy of about nine or ten.

Alison stared at the surprise on Duncan's face and then smiled.

"Ah, don't tell me. This is your first time, isn't it?"

Duncan looked from Alison to the boy's face and saw a reflection of himself. The boy's eyes bored into his own and Duncan knew the boy was the rogue.

"Hi, Dad," the boy said. "How long are you back for this time?"

Alison laughed at the expression on Duncan's face.

"You'd better come in," she said.

3.7 – Recriminations

"You idiot," Xander exploded.

Duncan stared into space.

"She called him Johnny," Duncan murmured.

"What a cliché," Xander snorted. "Anyway, the name's irrelevant. You must have passed on your genetics and now the damn kid has your access to the TC. He can link into it every bit as easily as we can."

"No, he's just feeling his way around it. He's not accessing it properly. That needs training."

Xander shook his head, the exasperated expression on his face a contrast to the bemused one Duncan wore. "He is why we can't get past 2002. I have no idea how but he has to be the reason there's no longer any future."

"But he can't be the real rogue, can he?" Duncan protested. "The one that was causing the kinks in the history timeline?"

"Why not? We haven't detected anything else."

Xander stopped and thought for a moment. "It's weird, but the disruption was getting stronger the closer we were getting set to come back here. The more certain we were to come back, the more pronounced the disruption became. Maybe if the mission had been cancelled, the disruptions would have faded as you wouldn't have been able to come back and, literally… well, to use a term common to this era, fuck it up in the first place."

"But that negates cause and effect. It's impossible."

"If we don't locate another rogue then you, Duncan, are the whole cause and effect."

"Hell, and I don't even remember having sexual relations with the woman. What are we going to do?" Duncan whispered.

Xander snarled, "Simple. We have to kill them."

Duncan's mouth dropped open.

3.8 – Howlaround

Obviously, the boy was far more in control of things than expected. Xander's initial plan had been to kill Alison before she gave birth but there was only a very small time window in which that could have been achieved. The boy had been conceived on the morning of September 1st 1968 and the TC hadn't appeared until the middle of May 1969. The boy had been born on May 24th whilst Alison was with her parents in Cornwall, far outside the range of the TC – they would have been hunting blind trying to find her out there.

So, they had to wait until Alison had come to London in August 1969. Her local doctor had booked an appointment at the Great Ormond Street Hospital for Sick Children to find out why the baby appeared to be having strange fits.

The TC registered the boy's presence as soon as he came within range and Xander decided to take the earliest opportunity to terminate the boy's life by whatever means possible. Duncan was also coming around to Xander's way of thinking. Day by day, he could see the local timeline deviating from the known path as the boy's future self gained experience in communicating with the TC.

They had tried to find a way to remove the boy's access to the device but, lacking anything other than a mental interface, they could not see how. It did what they wanted it to do, but it couldn't be persuaded to prevent the boy gaining similar access.

"Is he learning to time travel?" Duncan had asked when they were visiting 1989.

"No, that's the weird thing," Xander said. "He seems to be probing the TC and passing information about it back to his earlier self which, in turn, is augmenting his later self's abilities. It's some sort of closed self-reinforcing cycle, a feedback loop. I don't know how he's doing it but he is his own one-man chain reaction. Look at the number of times his signature is appearing between 1969 and 1990. When we first detected him there were only three signatures; now there are thousands. And it's all leaking out. Every time he reinforces his own timeline, something else gives. You've only got to look at the state of the country now to see how much worse the breakdown is becoming compared to when we first arrived."

Duncan nodded. A small matter of discontent in the 1980s had developed into riots and then open warfare on the streets. A few years earlier, a minor problem between the government and the trade unions had escalated into what had been termed the 'Winter of Discontent' in one timeline but, in a later one, it had morphed into the 'Winter of Complete Bloody Chaos.'

"Okay, you were right," Duncan admitted. "We've got to – stop him."

"No, not 'stop'. We've got to kill him. No half measures. Nothing short of his total obliteration will get us out of here."

So, they made a beeline for the Great Ormond Street Hospital in August 1969.

3.9 – A Slight Hitch In The Plan

In a panic, Duncan tried to staunch the flow of blood that oozed from various holes in Xander's head. There was more blood than he had cloth with which to wipe it up. Xander was still alive, but only just, and Duncan wasn't sure how long that life would remain.

A dilemma. He couldn't rely on the primitive skills of the 1969 medical profession and he couldn't risk trying to move Xander forwards thirty years to the slightly better but deteriorating facilities of 1999.

Xander had gone in quickly while the baby was being examined by a doctor with Alison waiting in a separate room. Xander had intended to materialise next to the child, kill him with a sharp knife, and exit as soon as possible. Duncan was to wait nearby as Xander knew he would be a liability, to which Duncan readily agreed.

What actually happened was that Xander was somehow diverted at speed about forty feet in the wrong direction. He materialised in a sterilising room, crashing against a trolley holding trays of surgical instruments, knocking it over and on top of himself as he fell. Several scalpels then found themselves embedded in his head. Duncan could feel the events unfolding, could see how the immature boy's mental power, guided by his own later influence, was taking control of events and distorting them to his own ends. Duncan had stepped into the room, avoiding the last of the falling scalpels, and dragged Xander across space, though not time, back to the lodgings.

Suddenly, Xander's eyes opened and Duncan saw the terror embedded within them. The TC had a moment when Duncan thought it was about to overload and then Xander fell quiet, eyes shut and the blood stopped oozing.

Then, as Xander's body faded from view, Duncan's connection with the TC faltered momentarily. When it returned, many of Xander's signatures had been erased. Of the two other very similar signatures, one was definitely becoming more numerous and far stronger.

3.10 – Seek And Ye Shall Find

After three unsuccessful attempts at diverting the timeline away from the one in which Xander was killed, Duncan realised he would have to find another method. He spent several months in accumulated time analysing the rickety state of the thirty years between when the TC arrived and the resultant end of the world. He made a number of discoveries but there were two that overarched all the others.

For a start, there was no longer just one disastrous timeline but a mash-up of hundreds, some more mangled than others. There were small snippets that were virtually untouched by the boy, especially after 1990. However, the devastation and events set in motion by his earlier influence were still causing the complete meltdown around ten years later. In these isolated snippets the world was almost as it would have been. Duncan retreated to one of the longer ones to do his studies, recycling his time over and over to reinforce his understanding of the situation. He also attempted to set up barriers within the TC to prevent the boy discovering him.

There were tracts, months long, within the late 1970s and early 1980s where the boy's power reigned and the TC was swamped with his presence. In between these were times, in more recent additions to the timeline, when the boy's power seemed diminished, narrowed somehow. It was within these that there seemed to be a shadow of something that was able to restrict the boy's influence upon the TC. Duncan knew he had to locate this shadow and find out what it was and how it worked.

After a few weeks he discovered that the shadow was leaving a new signature on the TC. One that was barely detectable because it was disguised as his own. It was piggybacking onto older existing signatures, subtly altering them and changing their impact. Did this mean that a new rogue had appeared? If so, then what were its intentions?

The more Duncan investigated how the signature overlays were being inserted, the more he came to understand how they worked. Then he realised that he could do the same thing himself and had a revelation. Some of the new signatures he'd discovered had started to disappear. Upon re-inserting them they punched back through the timelines to the earlier state when he had first discovered them. He shook his head as understanding dawned – cause and effect had been reversed. His later self had taught his earlier self how to do something new – so where had the idea come from? This was inconceivable – it couldn't possibly be happening, but it was.

For a while he wavered on the verge of inaction, scared that what he was doing could bring the whole of reality crashing down. Then he figured that the boy was already doing this himself. So, he knew he had to continue.

Fired up, he became bolder, introducing an overlay onto a signature for an event in 1981. He examined the timeline from the original event, where the boy had cut his hand on a kitchen knife during the late morning of 21st January 1981. His rage had rippled out and eventually caused an attempt on the life of the Prime Minister when she'd visited the USA the following month. Duncan examined his own timeline for the 21st January and chose an event just prior to the knife event where he purchased a newspaper at Victoria Railway Station. He then travelled back to Alison's house while it was unoccupied and subtly changed the placement of the knife in the kitchen drawer so that the boy would no longer cut his hand. He then merged the signatures of the two events into one so that only the original newspaper buying event was prominent, though it also held the other event within it. The change was immediate and the assassination attempt was eliminated from the timeline.

Finally, he was onto something.

3.11 – Loading The Gun

Duncan spent several more weeks with the overlays, each one a minor success, but, in the grand scheme of things, doing very little to change the final outcome. He needed another method of attack. He also needed to cauterise the rest of the world from Johnny's influence, to prune the boy's actions back to a restricted, manageable range.

It took a while – in total, more than ten years of personal, overlapped time.

During this age he crafted new overlays, interlinking each one within a web that tied the boy down harder with every new addition but securely linking it to others to prevent their subsequent undoing. He watched the boy's effect on the timeline gradually start to diminish and become contained. Five years in and Duncan had removed the boy's ability to directly manipulate anything past the mid-eighties. He watched the timelines shift and reconfigure as the holocaust of the late nineties reduced themselves back to normal non-nuclear war. Seven years in and there were hints that dates past 2002 were starting to become viable again. It took another nine months to understand that the future was secured.

But tackling the boy himself was becoming harder. The more Duncan restricted his actions, the more Johnny's influence on the 1970s exerted itself. He had difficulty preventing the boy undoing or perverting the fixes and changes he made in that decade. Almost as soon as a set of fixes were installed, the boy would bring them toppling down with another change.

The breakthrough came when Duncan remembered he could set triggers – incidents that could be forced to occur when other events had come to pass. It was not a common technique, and certainly not one that he had personally found useful on previous missions. He spent a week immersed in the TC's learning mode while he re-acquired the rusty skills that had hardly been more than a class exercise when he'd originally been taught them.

Once familiarity was gained, he set about engineering a new interlinked web that would propagate both up and down the thirty year range and, if it worked, would restore the world to normality. Upon initiation it would be like a line of rapidly falling dominoes. Hopefully, the boy wouldn't have time to devise a method of preventing their completion. He tested the outcome of each addition via the speculative prediction circuits of the TC. How accurate the TC could be was, of course, conjecture. But it was all he had.

It wasn't the only problem. To trigger such a cascade required a huge initial event, and Duncan needed to be at the centre of the action. So close that the outcome of undoing everything his son had accomplished would be extremely costly. He explored alternatives but, according to the prediction circuits, nothing other than the most expensive would achieve the desired result.

He sighed, accepting the outcome knowing there was no way to cheat this himself – the whole disaster had been his own doing, he knew he had to finish it properly.

One consolation was that he found that he could add an extra twist that could yet give his apparently deceased companion a slim chance. Given the turmoil immediately connected with Xander's demise, his death was still not a completely fixed event. Duncan knew he had to do what he could.

At last, it was all done and he was ready. He had run through the prediction circuits until the preferred outcome resulted with a nearly one-hundred percent accuracy each time. Finally, he added the signature that activated everything and then transported himself across London and back to 1979.

3.12 – Pulling The Trigger

Having materialised a safe distance away, Duncan picked his way amongst the debris of the once respectable suburban street. He could sense disparate timelines phasing in and out, and vying for reality. The whole area was unstable.

That wasn't all – this close to his target, the area was littered with burnt out vehicles, scuttling rats and overgrown gardens. The corruption was layered and piled high. He hoped that what he had put in place could undo all of this. He reached the centre, and walked up the pathway of the now familiar house. He remembered doing this before, on this exact same date. On that occasion, now lost in the rearranging time stream, the street had looked normal and the boy had only just discovered the TC.

Duncan's feet found the glass of a broken milk bottle in the porch. A dead blue tit lay amongst the shards.

He swallowed and rapped on the door, avoiding the screwdriver that, for some reason, was embedded in the wood. He heard movement inside and, a few seconds later, the door opened an inch before being swung fully wide.

"Oh. Hi, Duncan," Alison said. "Come in. It's getting worse out there."

Duncan entered the house and then paused beside the woman. What, he wondered, had happened to the willowy, blonde girl from the Isle of Wight? This version of Alison was overweight, with hair that was both wild and dark. Her eyes had the haunted look of someone who had seen far too much. His own were probably the same.

He paused and smiled at her before kissing her on the cheek. There was a movement near the top of the stairs. Nine-year-old Johnny peered at him with an expression of pure hatred. You, my boy, Duncan thought, don't realise what you've got yourself into. I have come to take you down, and take you down I will.

But, what he actually said to the boy was, "Hi Johnny, how's Natalie?"

A frown furrowed Alison's face – she was, in this time, unaware of anyone called Natalie. Her frown was cut off by the expletives that erupted from above. Duncan chuckled to himself as Johnny rushed back up onto the landing. A squeal from the kitchen was followed by the appearance of Matilda, still more pig than cat, chasing a mouse along the hallway.

He put his arm around Alison's waist and steered the woman towards the foot of the stairs. He winked at her and whispered, "Make sure we're not disturbed."

She grinned back in anticipation and called up to Johnny, "It's time for your bed. Now, and no argument."

Duncan felt the TC acknowledge a new restriction fall into place about the boy and then laughed as Johnny screamed in rage, slamming his bedroom door shut. The reverberation echoed back into the past and Duncan, grabbing Alison, followed it to 1975.

As he led Alison up the stairs to the bedroom he felt the TC's predictions falling into place.

Part 1b – Affect

1.3b – What Really Happened

Outside the module, Preston pressed a button and a howl reverberated around the room. Inside the module, the gut-wrenching started and the contents of the module were catapulted over six hundred years into the past to land in 1970 or thereabouts

After the noise died down Preston opened the door to make sure it was as empty as expected.

It wasn't.

In the right hand seat Xander was screaming and clutching at his face as if he was trying to remove things that penetrated his skull.

What Preston saw in the left hand seat was even worse. It wasn't just that Duncan appeared years older, it was more to do with the large hole in his side from which blood had exploded. His lower body was soaked with it.

Preston punched at a keyboard, figures blazed across a screen and confirmed that Duncan was either dead or not far from it. Preston hit the emergency button and, while he waited for the crew to arrive and deal with the mess, removed the TC from the module.

He plugged it into an interface slot and then tried to get some readings from it.

It contradicted itself.

1.4 – Post Mortem

"They couldn't have travelled anywhere," Preston said for the third time. "There just wasn't time for the whole sequence."

It was twenty-four hours since the return, and they were still unsure about what had gone wrong.

"Yet the TC is crammed with data," Charles Alton argued. "It must have come from somewhere."

One of Alton's assistants entered the room after a brief knock at the door. "Erm, excuse me, but the problem appears to have resolved itself. The nineteen seventies are back on track. They must have succeeded."

Alton let out a sigh and made eye contact with Preston, who raised his eyebrows.

Preston shook his head, "Well, I have never experienced a sending and return so close together. Technically, they should be two completely separate events."

Alton nodded and countered, "However, it happened, they went, they came back. And one is dead and the other so deranged it's uncertain he'll ever recover."

Preston was forced to agree. "So. What does the TC analysis give us?"

It was Alton's turn to sigh. "There is so much data in there, much of it completely unlike anything we've ever seen or simulated before. It will take years

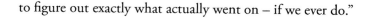

to figure out exactly what actually went on – if we ever do."

The Paradox Engineers *had quite a long gestation period. What became part two – the 'Boiled Insurance Salesman' section – was written in 2008 but those reading it hadn't really understood the concept of someone experiencing changing timelines in a completely fractured manner. So, in 2015, I wrapped the original section within a longer piece, giving it a more solid reason for its existence.*

Stopped

Everything stopped.

No, that is a lie.

Except for myself, everyone and everything stopped.

Yes, that is less of a lie.

They stopped. Whatever they were doing, they stopped doing it and lay down. It didn't matter if they were working, playing, riding a bike or walking the dog. They stopped. They just stopped; they lay down where they were and stopped. They didn't fall, they didn't clutch their chests and collapse – they just lay down and stopped.

And I?

On a normal Saturday morning, walking through the city crowds, only I failed to stop. I just stood transfixed, mouth dangling open while all around me the world slowly stopped.

For a while I wondered about planes falling from the sky, about power stations exploding due to people not being there. But, as far as I can tell, these things never happened. Maybe they just stopped as well, wherever they were.

Nature too.

The days pass but each feels the same. Trees that still sway in the breeze fail to grow taller. Grass no longer needs cutting. Flowers bloom forever, their petals as devoid of bees as their stems are of ants. The sky is empty of birds, bats and flying insects.

Now no one works, eats, talks, plays or laughs. No one walks their dog for their dogs are as immobile as they.

Yet, no one actually sleeps – for what they do can no longer be described as sleeping. It is not death – a coma perhaps? How can I tell? I was never a doctor.

You could, if you were so inclined, rest your ear against a person's chest. After a while, after a very long while, you might think you detect the occasional slow beat of the heart, the almost random rise and fall of the rib cage as a rare breath is taken.

Of course, if you wait around long enough, you would notice something even more profound, something even stranger. And that is that no one passes away. Despite the lack of food and water, the people do not die; they do not slowly dry out, their skin does not stiffen and shrink, their muscles do not diminish, their flesh does not crumble and fall from their bones. They remain as they were when they stopped.

They just are.

But will they always be so?

You will have to wait a long time to find out. I know I have. And what have I found?

Maybe, once in a while, you would imagine that one of these people twitched or moved a finger or swallowed. I know I do.

But would you be right? Would it have happened? Or would it be something only seen from the corner of your eye? I have seen them blink, smile and twitch but I have seen none of these things directly. Only on the shadowy edge of my vision do they perform such actions – never in plain view.

And why do I even speak to you about these things as if you are really here, as if you can hear my words, as if you are as real as me?

I know you are nothing but a figment of my age-old imagination. I conjure you up to talk to; to be a companion – my only companion. The imaginary imaginings of a senile old man.

And all around me are my former companions – none moving, none sleeping, none being.

And I ask the same questions over again.

Why did this happen? Why did I escape their fate? Why did I not escape my own? As all the rest of my world fell into prolonged silence, why did only I do no such thing?

How many years have passed since they stopped? I cannot tell for I am beyond counting. Once, I did count. Once I kept records for as long as I could. I marked the days, the months, the years, the decades, the centuries. But finally they became meaningless. What do centuries mean to someone who cannot die?

Ah, death – that welcome ender of nightmares. How I long for an end to my own nightmare. But, the nightmare never ceases. Not that I haven't, many times, tried to force an end.

No, I cannot die. I have tried by means simple and complicated to terminate this existence. And all fail. I will not bore you with the detail of my attempts though, in desperation, some were beyond any horror I could have previously imagined. But all were in vain, and in pain I endure until I heal. And, after I heal, then I carry on watching the stopped.

I am fated to live as those around me fail to live.

Sometimes I suspect that their life has passed to me – and it is I who must live, must move, must breathe, must sleep for them.

And maybe I must finish living all of their lives before I myself can finally stop.

A nightmare situation – I no longer recall exactly what inspired **Stopped***, which was penned in 2007.*

The Long Ago Now

My fingers hovered beside but hesitated to touch the structure. Inside the transparent casing the metal wheels, cogs and other parts of the movement still shone as if they had been made yesterday. They appeared static, but the occasional clunk from within the chamber hinted otherwise. By some miracle the machine still worked. I wondered what the builders had looked like.

It had been hard to find. We had come down over the planet days before and had not expected to find evidence of previous occupation. We'd swooped low over the terrain, marvelling at the creatures that roamed the plains, that were hidden in jungles and swam freely in the oceans. They had been plentiful, more so than back home. Even when home had still been young, before our greed had diminished it to its current state. Now, of course, we had to find a new home to replace our own plundered planet.

Then the ship's computers dashed the hope that this world would provide the answer for which we hunted.

"There is evidence of a previous civilisation," we were told, once the probes had done their work. We looked at the evidence and it was old. Older than some of the hills, if we read the data correctly.

The co-pilot said, "The ground has been stripped of much of the resources."

I sighed. Whoever had occupied this world had gone down the same path as ourselves. At least we had managed to reach the stars, apparently something that the creatures here had never achieved.

The probes had barely detected the remaining fragments of their cities, hidden beneath desert or drowned in the sea.

Then, when we were almost ready for departure, they found the device in a mountain. On one of the land masses, which had remained relatively unscathed throughout the unknown period between the now and when this world had teemed with intelligence, there was still a remnant. Below the mountain's flanks the prairie teemed with beasts. Some were similar while others were far unlike those I recall from our own world. One species, surprisingly, ran about on two legs while their forelimbs gyrated about their heads for no apparent reason. Herds of the strange creatures stampeded as the ship swung over their heads as we came in to land.

The two of us donned our protective suits and stepped outside. The local star was almost overhead and its heat baked the land about us. As captain I was first to venture inside the mountain through the lower of two entrances the probes had detected. An airlock prevented the intrusion of wildlife and I immediately felt the heat from outside fall away. I was in a vertical chamber whose spiral steps wound their way upwards through the rock. Beyond a certain point a continuous breeze passed by me. I queried this with the computers and it determined that the breeze was being used as a power source.

That intrigued me – a power source for what?

Eventually, I reached the main mechanism. It was crude in its simplicity and yet magnificent in its resilience. On all the planet only this remained standing as evidence that minds other than ours had once risen above the mediocre and managed to fashion something lasting. How long it had stood on this spot was still being questioned by the ship's computers.

Then came the noise – had I tripped an alarm? Apparently not, as the jangle of deep tones seemed to present no danger. After a while they stopped and I continued upwards.

I scanned the mechanism and the computers interpreted the detail within the resultant data. It returned the verdict that the mechanism was a clock. The noises I heard were, I was informed, an indication that the local star had reached a particular point of the day. As the star had passed the zenith by a short period, the computers suggested that the clock's timekeeping had drifted. This may have been due to the various intolerances in its construction or even possibly a small change in the period at which the planet rotated since the device had been built.

I explored other parts of the cavern system. There were chambers that may once have held information or artifacts, but there was little left other than dust.

Later on, I returned to the ship and the co-pilot pushed it up and out of the atmosphere. We compared notes and, over dinner, speculated on what we had found.

"At least," I said, "we have the knowledge that we're no longer alone in the universe. Even though these creatures are extinct, it is an indisputable fact that they became advanced enough to build themselves a civilisation."

The co-pilot replied, "They got at least as far as the local satellite."

He showed me footage of some artifacts a probe had discovered on the large grey rock that orbited this world. It depicted an angular structure that appeared to have toppled over onto its side. Nearby was a piece of material. Although faded almost to pure white, closer analysis detected that it had once contained three colours. These colours had been used to depict red and white stripes with a smaller blue rectangle containing a number of small white-pointed shapes.

I wondered what it meant.

The **Long Ago Now** *was written in 2013 after reading about the* **The Long Now Foundation** *and the clock they are building. You can find out more at:*
   https://longnow.org

Ten Minutes

They sat on fold-up chairs gazing out through a window at an ocean. It filled the horizon. Having arrived less than ten minutes previously, they wondered what the event would be this time.

They were in a small, unfurnished and unoccupied house. Between them on the floor sat a machine that gave off a hum. There were two clocks on one side of the machine – the larger one said 5:42 and the smaller read 14:42 – it was mid afternoon, so the smaller one was right. Five cameras attached by wires to the machine recorded the view out the window and inside the room.

"Been on many of these, Ted? This is my twenty-third," the younger man said.

The older man chuckled, "Hundreds, Jack. Lost count."

Jack seemed impressed by this. "How long you been doing it, then?"

This was the first time these two had been paired together for a mission. Ted sighed, he wasn't one for small talk. "Nineteen-thirties. I was twenty-five. Got sent to Nazi Germany a few times. Minor stuff, nothing you'd remember."

"Wow." Jack was even more impressed. "I got recruited in the late eighties but they pushed me up several years as they were short of people in this time, apparently."

"Yeah, I missed much of the eighties and nineties – same reason. At least I always know exactly where I was when Kennedy kicked it, and I wasn't sitting on a grassy knoll." The old man chuckled again, but the joke seemed to go over the younger man's head.

"Have you ever seen one of the bosses?" Jack asked to cover his ignorance.

"Of course not. As far as I can tell, no one has. I know a few who tried – like my last partner."

"What happened?"

"Try it and you don't work for them any more. Like, you don't work. Period."

Ted's face hardened, his lips thinned.

Embarrassed, Jack looked back out over the ocean. Along the coast to the right there was a large industrial complex – it resembled a power station or something, not that the younger man was an expert in such things. They had been sent to observe an event somewhere around the world – he consulted his electronic pad, it said Japan. The view out the window could have been anywhere on any coast. All they had to do was make sure that both they and the machine experienced and observed it, and then the machine would bring them back. It was a bit like being a journalist but you never had to sit around for hours waiting for something to happen. With this job, there was always an event to cover.

"Nothing I've covered was really that interesting," Jack mused. "Best one was when I was sent to witness a plane crash in the Bahamas in 2001 – some woman singer I never heard of got killed. You covered anything like that?"

Ted sighed again, wishing Jack would shut up. However, he dredged his memory before saying, "Yeah. Buddy Holly, 9/11, a bunch of English footballers in the sixties, Concorde in France in 2000 – plenty of 'em and that was just the plane crashes."

There was silence between them for a few seconds while Jack took it all in. Out the window the ocean could be seen gently rolling its waves towards the land.

Then everything changed.

The whole room rocked. The window shattered accompanied by the sound of glass breaking elsewhere. The building creaked and threatened to collapse.

"Bloody hell," Jack screeched as he was flung from his chair. His hands automatically covered his face as he crashed into the machine.

"Watch out," Ted shouted as he attempted to pick himself up from the floor. "Another earthquake. Should've known, being Japan. Not a lot else happens here apart from the odd bomb and killing whales and dolphins. Damn, it's a big one. Help me fix those cameras properly."

They stumbled about the room, trying to avoid broken glass and resiting the devices that had toppled from where they had been placed. The rumbling persisted for over five minutes before it began to subside.

"I think you'd better look at this," Jack said, peering at the machine. "There's some lights flashing."

Ted examined red lights that glowed brightly for a moment before fading away. The machine stopped humming.

"Oh, bloody typical," he sighed. "It's busted. Now we've got to wait for someone to come and get us."

"Will that take long?" Jack had a tremor in his voice. He glanced out the window to where the ocean was decidedly less calm.

"Yeah, no problem. I've had four or five of the damned things die on me. They're programmed to return at a certain time and, if they don't, an alarm goes off back at base ten minutes later. Sometimes you think they're built like tanks, then you sneeze and the bloody things fall to pieces. Crap alien tech."

"How long are we due to stay here?"

"It's on your pad."

Jack's fingers shook as he tried to locate the information.

Damned kids, Ted thought and then regretted it; he had been young once. Now here he was in… he tapped at his own pad… March 2011 having only aged less than half the number of years that had passed since they'd recruited him.

"Um, we were due to return at 15:48 local time. That's about an hour, isn't it?" Jack said.

Ted checked the clocks on the machine – neither was running. His own watch bore no relation to the local time, it said 10:27.

"Okay," he said. "Looks like we'll be picked up at around four o'clock then – half eleven-ish by my watch."

They moved to the window. Even though the machine was dead, they still had a duty to observe any ongoing events. Ted pulled some shattered glass from the frame and watched it drop to the ground below. The sea was still choppy and, in the distance, they could hear alarms going off. There were few people around – the observation site had been chosen for its remoteness, to prevent anyone local noticing either themselves or their equipment.

"Why was the recall time so long after the earthquake?" Jack asked.

"They do that sometimes when something else is about to happen."

"How do they know?"

"They say the bosses can time travel backwards from the future even though they only let us go forwards. I reckon they don't trust us not to introduce any paradoxes."

The time crept past slowly until it was about twenty minutes from the time Ted thought they might be picked up.

"Look at the sea," Jack said. But Ted had already noticed the tide receding. The shoreline retreated rapidly into the distance leaving fish and debris stranded.

He whistled. "Never seen that before. Very weird."

They continued to observe.

"I reckon now was when we should have gone back. About ten minutes to go. We can probably stop observing now."

But they continued to watch. The clouds were becoming thicker and darker out at sea, and the tide had started to return.

Ted checked his watch – it read 11:21. The alarm would have been raised at the base by now. In the distance they could hear the squealing of yet more local alarms. He wondered what they signified.

"Is that normal?" Jack said, pointing at the horizon.

Ted squinted, his older eyes initially unable to detect the dark line. Then it came into focus – it was racing closer, rapidly. After a minute they both realised what it was.

A tsunami.

"Shit!" they both shouted in unison.

Sometimes alien tech can be almost as bad as terran tech! **Ten Minutes** *was originally written in 2013 about a year and a half after the devastating event it portrays.*

Love Will Prevail

Pain in my chest, arms, shoulders.

I think, 'This is probably it,' as the wave of nausea spreads. But, after a few minutes, the pain subsides and I rock in the chair, light-headed and short of breath.

My eyes refocus again, and see the small plot of tilled land in front of me, the slope down to the cliff edge and, beyond that, the blue of the English Channel.

For perhaps the thousandth time I think I should have written my life down. But who would read it? If I'd realised I would live this long then maybe I would have done so. Now, almost with relief, I know it's too late.

As I sit there gasping, my eyes watch gulls circle in the air beyond the cliffs. Farther west an animal, a wild cat or maybe a fox, runs along what was once a road.

I didn't realise I was special until they took me away. I was twelve. Home was a semi in London's western suburbs with my aged parents and an older, infertile sister.

Dad answered the knock at the door. Two men in suits entered without invitation. The smaller one said, "Congratulations. Daniel is fertile. May we see him?"

They'd only tested me a few days beforehand.

Mum pushed me forward but I felt embarrassed under the gaze of these strangers. The large man held my arm.

"He is to come with us immediately," said the smaller man. Dad appeared shocked. Mum started to protest but the larger man led me away to a car. Before the car door imprisoned me, I heard my mother's hysterics echoing along the street.

I didn't know it then but that would be the last time I'd ever see my family.

In a state of shock I was driven into the countryside. After two, maybe three hours we stopped at a building. It was so old it had been built with red bricks. Some of the windows were broken. I was led inside and my footfalls echoed in the corridors. There were rows of empty desks in some of the rooms. The dust lay thick upon them. It looked as if it had once been a school.

Only one room was being used – about fifteen girls were being taught by an old woman of maybe thirty-five. After a brief halt I was taken to see another, even older woman.

"About time," she said. "They promised us a fertile boy months ago."

"Rare as hen's teeth," said the smaller man.

"Only twelve though," she sighed, inspecting me. "He doesn't look old enough, does he? We'll start the testosterone treatment immediately. At least they sent that through quickly enough." She turned to the man and said, "You know some of the fifteen-year-olds are already starting to hit menopause?"

"Jesus," he said. "Last I heard the earliest was seventeen."

"They kept the recent drop quiet. Fertility will soon be down to a couple of years at the most."

"Did you hear they've dropped the age of 'consent' again?" the man said.

"Yes, ridiculous isn't it. Anyway, they don't consent, we make them do it."

"It's the only way," the man sighed.

They made me strip and, after making more comments about my lack of development, injected me in the buttocks. It hurt and I whimpered. After being allowed to dress, I was made to join the class of girls. A few may have been younger than me but most appeared older. They were being taught mathematics – it was vaguely familiar to me but I couldn't concentrate under the stares of the girls.

It took me only a short while to realise that I was the only boy at the school. I was given a room of my own and new clothes, along with weekly injections. They made me ill.

However, over the next few months I did start developing quickly. During that time three of the older girls left the school and one younger girl joined.

I raise myself from the rocking chair on the porch and, bent over, shuffle back inside the bungalow. A bout of nausea hits and I clutch at the door frame to prevent myself falling. Gasping, I watch peeling paint flutter to the ground. In the kitchen I collapse onto a chair. A while later I am able to pour water from a bottle into a glass and tip it down my throat. The pain is almost gone but I am weak and shaking. The bottle is nearly empty – I need to pump more from the well, but why should I bother?

Glancing through the door into the lounge my eyes fall upon the short wave radio. Should I try it again tonight? No, there's no point. The batteries are running down and I haven't the strength to clean the solar panels that charge them. Anyway, I haven't found anyone to speak to for months.

A song comes into my head, a popular one from when I was a boy of seven or eight – nearly thirty-five years ago. I can't remember all the words now – but the chorus went, 'The Earth will reject us, Love will prevail.' – I didn't know what it meant when I was young.

I do now.

One day, after I'd been at the school for about eight months, the teacher said it was time for sex education.

"Come to the front, Daniel," the teacher said. I did so. "Remove your clothes." When I hesitated, she dragged the clothes from my body. Several of the girls sniggered at my nakedness.

"Quiet," the teacher ordered. "Now, who is at the peak of their cycle?" After a hesitation, four girls raised their hands. The teacher's eyes skipped over three of them and came to rest upon the eldest. "Amber, bring your chart here."

Amber, two years older than I, approached the teacher and handed her a sheet of paper. The teacher examined it.

"If this is accurate, you should be at your peak tomorrow. Now is good enough, though. Strip."

She did so, without delay, and the teacher seemed pleased to see my reaction to Amber's nakedness. Then she showed me what to do – it was embarrassing but the teacher seemed pleased. She also collected the residue, sucked it up into three eye-dropper tubes and gave it to the other three girls.

"You know what to do with that?"

The girls nodded.

In the cool of the late evening I rest in the darkness. Lying on the tattered sofa, I have decided it's too much effort to go to bed. My heartbeat feels irregular and I keep expecting the pain to return. My hand rests on the radio. I toy with the idea of trying it again but exhaustion clamps me to my place. So I think back to my youth.

Six girls became pregnant that first year, though only five managed to produce live offspring. And one of those died not long after birth. They were soon tested and I was informed that two of them, both girls, were likely to be fertile. They and their mothers were taken away.

Both babies from the second year were born infertile – there were a few more pregnancies but no more live babies after that. At fifteen I was still the only boy and there were only four girls left. No new girls had arrived for over a year.

"Your sperm count is hardly measurable, Daniel. It's pointless you being here any more," the teacher said with a sigh. It was just a few weeks after my sixteenth birthday. The wrinkles on the teacher's face had multiplied over the past four years. She was nearing forty and needed a stick to get around as arthritis ravaged her shrivelled body.

"You're free to go," she added and her gaze wandered to the window where two of the remaining girls were working in the vegetable garden. She seemed to forget I was there.

"What will I do?" I asked, wanting to break the silence.

"Do?" The question appeared to surprise her. She thought for a while. "Anything you want, I suppose. Go back to your family."

I turned to leave the room.

"You were probably the last, you know. There's no point now, anyway. Menopause sets in only a month after puberty. No point to anything, any more."

I got a lift back to London from Gerald, a man in his late twenties. Gerald made a living driving stuff about for others. He owned an electric van powered by solar cells and held together with bodged repairs. He taught me how to drive it and, for a while, I helped him clear out empty houses and sell on the contents. There were more empty houses every day. When I found it at last, the home I'd grown up in was also empty – it was obvious it had been deserted for years.

One day, when I was twenty-four, Gerald collapsed. No hospital would take him as they said he was too old – he was thirty-five. So I tried searching the internet but so much of that had gone and there were no answers. I cared for Gerald until he died. Then I carried on doing what he had done. There was nothing else, other than trying to grow food, of course. I managed to keep the van going for a few years repairing it as Gerald had taught me.

There came a time, not long after, when I heard there were no more fertile people left in the world. It may have been true, I don't know. I also heard that the world population was down to under a billion. That may have been true as well. I did know that the oldest people alive were only in their early forties.

As the dawn comes up I switch on the radio for a while. There are probably only a few minutes of use before the batteries completely drain. I move the dial from one end to the other but hear only static. I am too weak to use the microphone.

I haven't heard a human voice in months. The last was a man in his late thirties from somewhere in Eastern Europe, his broken English informing me that he was the last person alive in his town or village.

When the sun comes up fully I find the strength to wheeze out of the bungalow and sit in the rocking chair. The exertion leaves my chest tight, and my breathing quick and shallow. I wonder again how many others are left. Maybe I really am the last.

As usual, gulls fly out over the sea and birds sing in the wildness. That same wildness encroaches onto my pathetic patch of garden. Soon there will be no evidence that I'd ever tilled this land, that I'd ever planted carrots, beans, lettuces and tomatoes.

After a while a stabbing pain flows along my arm and I close my eyes hoping for release. Again that song comes back to haunt me – "The Earth will reject us."

Not quite right, I thought. It already has.

*In **Love Will Prevail**, which was written in 2011, I deliberately decided not to go into the exact cause of the catastrophic decline in human fertility and longevity. That no cure has been discovered is implied, though never stated. The title itself comes from a never completed song written back in the 1980s.*

Jumper

On Tuesday 5th June 2001 I wake up wearing different pyjamas to the ones I was sure I put on last night. I get up and go downstairs to find my house full of strangers. Well, not strangers, exactly.

"Hi Dad. Hah – you look well confused."

The girl appears to be about eighteen. Another, a couple of years younger says, "Oh God, I'd forgotten about that moustache."

"He shaves it off in a few days, his time."

The woman who spoke is my wife. Only she isn't. Not my wife, that is – not the Jennifer I went to bed with last night. This one is older, her face carries lines I've never seen before and her hair, shorter than yesterday, has fine streaks of grey.

"Sit down," she says. "I've cooked your favourite breakfast."

The smell of bacon and eggs hits me as the plate hits the table and, meekly, I sit before it and stare. I am not hungry.

"What…" I begin.

"We've taken the day off. All of us," says my nearly wife. "Well, it is your first trip. Bit special this one."

"Dad, it's okay. It really is us," the younger girl says. I stare at her and can see that it is my youngest daughter, only grown up. "I'm sixteen now."

"Ruby?"

"Yes, and it's me, Jessica," says the elder girl with a hint of sarcasm.

Somehow I see that it's true.

"How?"

"You time travelled," Ruby says, unhelpfully.

"How?" I repeat.

"Who knows." Jessica, this time. "It's Thursday the tenth of March, twenty-eleven."

"Twenty-eleven? Two thousand and eleven?"

"Yep."

"How…?"

"We don't know, honey. We – that is, you and me, sometime back in 2001 – decided that it was better we didn't tell people. They'd probably have locked you up or something. Me too, possibly. So we never did… and you won't."

With the smell of bacon and eggs drifting into my nose I stare out the window. The back garden has changed; less neat, trees taller. A cat I've never seen before rubs against my ankle.

"Sookey knows it's still you," Ruby says, reaching down to tickle the animal behind its ear.

"What happened to Pixie?"

"Under the rose." Jessica points out the window and I see some pruned twigs sticking out of the ground. They may have once been a rose bush. "She was really old, even back then."

I start crying. I can't help it. This is too strange. Somehow I've lost ten years. Amnesia?

Jenny puts her arms around my shoulders. "Hey, it's okay, love. You'll be back home tomorrow after a good sleep. That's the way it works."

"What?"

"Right now, the you who was here yesterday is back in 2001 and scaring the shit out of me and the girls. The only difference is that he was expecting it and you weren't – you being here, that is. And tomorrow you'll both be back where you belong. You back then and him back here. Simple as that. Now, eat your breakfast. It's the first time I've made a fry-up in years."

She was right. It's now the next day – the proper next day. Last night I went to bed with a woman nearly ten years older than me and now it all seems like a bad dream. I'm home again with a younger wife and daughters who are still only six and eight. However, they are staring at me as if they are not sure who or what I am.

It was no dream, then.

I'm sitting in bed holding a sheet of paper containing a list of dates – pairs of them – written in my own hand. But I didn't write them. Jenny says they were written yesterday by my future self. The dates fill the page – fifty seven pairs of them. How could I have remembered such a long list?

"That really was you yesterday?" Jenny asks. I see the worry lines on her face, echoes of the permanent lines to come.

"I think so, yes. What did he say?"

"Well, I screamed at first. Which made the girls cry. You, er, he explained but I couldn't understand. I still don't…"

I shake my head in agreement. I don't understand either but obviously my future wife had come – will come to accept it. And looking on the bright side I can confidently predict that my marriage will last at least ten years longer and that my children will grow up without mishap. Not all husbands and fathers would be lucky enough to have a guarantee like that.

Jenny cries and I comfort her. On the list I notice that the first pair of dates are 15/6/2001 and 10/3/2011 – yesterday and the day I travelled to. All the other dates lie in between those two, listed in order of the first date. Some pairs are only weeks apart. The next pair are 4/8/2001 and 27/5/2004, which means I have about seven weeks before I travel to just under three years into the future.

Why me? And how?

Madness, but I can see why I – we – decided or will decide, perhaps, not to tell anyone about this. Even if I did tell, how many times would it take before they would actually believe me?

A few days later I stare at my reflection in the mirror and decide it's time to shave off my moustache. Jenny says I look better without it.

I am standing in the lounge talking to the future Jenny late one night when my vision blurs and I flip over onto my back, my t-shirt and trousers are immediately replaced by pyjamas. I wake up in bed without having been asleep. The effect is unnerving.

After three such occurrences I have an inkling that the jumps are always initiated by whichever version of myself is furthest in the past. I suspect they also happen not long after I fall asleep. I have no clue as to whether or not such information is significant.

"I don't remember winning, so therefore," I argue, "I could never have done it."

"But maybe you kept it secret," twelve-year-old Jessica insists.

It's a day before I am due to skip back a few weeks and Jessica has got this idea that I should memorise last week's winning lottery numbers. But I know I didn't and I find the idea dangerous. Whatever is causing these jumps might take offence at me meddling with history even on such a small personal scale.

Jessica pouts at such potential loss of wealth.

It's March the eleventh, 2011. The last jump has been and gone. It was hard remembering all those dates for the last trip. But I managed it as I knew I would.

And now it's over. No more time travelling. I go to bed confident in a future that will finally occur in the correct sequence.

It's a pity I was wrong.

I awake on a floor lacking a carpet in a room devoid of furniture. Not even a complete room. Where there was once a wall and bedroom window there is now a gap. Above me most of the roof is gone.

Sand and grit layer the floor. My fingers find bare floorboards below the sand, the wood worn smooth. The air is hot and dry, and a wind continuously keeps the sand in motion.

I push myself to my feet and the remaining tatters of pyjamas fall from my body. I pick up a piece of the cloth and it disintegrates between my finger and thumb. The fragments merge with the shifting sand.

Beyond the shattered house is a desert punctuated by the remains of buildings. Across the road – or where a road may still lie beneath the sand – I can recognise the general outline of the house that has always been there. But the one in my memory has a sweeping drive and is framed by conifers taller than the house itself. This one has no accompanying conifers or even a recognisable garden.

I inch down the rotten staircase, jumping the last couple of feet where stairs no longer exist. My bare feet slip into the sand, hot and itchy between my toes. I am thirsty. The kitchen – or what was once the kitchen – lacks not only furniture but also plumbing.

The rest of the house contains nothing but sand. There is no water. There are no clothes. Even the wallpaper has been stripped away from the walls.

What year is this? I have no way of determining an answer. It could be 2012, 2021, 2061 or 3011 for all I can tell. It doesn't matter – I just need to survive a few hours until sleep overtakes me again.

We live not far from the river and I head in that direction hoping to find a trickle. A valley in the dunes shows where it once ran but there is no water; not even a dampness to the sand. I find shade from the sun and wind behind a building and spend the day there, parched, hot and desperate. As the sun begins to set I head back towards my house. A moment of panic overcomes me when I fear I cannot re-locate it but, exhausted, eventually I do.

The fragility of the stairs prevents a return to the bedroom. Instead, I haul myself through into what was once the lounge and collapse into a less exposed corner that's almost out of the wind. The day's heat slides away to be replaced by a cold, star-filled night.

I bury myself in the sand to keep warm and close my eyes, knowing I need to sleep in order to wrench myself back to the reality of 2011. But the wind and cold prevent slumber for what seems like hours. And then I do sleep and I dream of home, of Jennifer, Jessica and Ruby and of telling them of my adventure in a future world.

But when I awake to the beginnings of a new day, the desert still surrounds me.

There is a residue of dew on my body. Such a tiny amount is nectar and, as I try to get as much into my mouth as possible, my head attempts to analyse what has gone wrong. If I am here then what version of me went back to lay in my bed? I imagine Jennifer's horror upon awakening to find the remains of a skeleton in the bed beside her.

Is that what happened?

But, if I can't return, then what was wearing the pyjamas before I arrived? Paradox haunts every possibility I consider. No matter which way I try to work it out, I can't make it add up.

By the time the sun sets, my thoughts are whirling with impossible ideas and thirst wracks my body with pain.

I don't remember sleeping but awake again to a third day. I have neither the inclination nor the strength to make use of the dew that has settled once more upon my skin. The heat rises, the dew dissipates but I am now immune to the thirst. My skin has taken on a shrivelled aspect that part of my mind finds almost amusing.

One of the last coherent thoughts I have is that, maybe, I didn't jump in time, but went sideways into some alternative dimension. So, did a substitute version of me take my place?

As darkness overwhelms me I pray, for Jennifer's sake, that this might be true.

Having written **Underneath The Arches**, *a time travel story where music would initiate a jump, I wondered what might happen if a past and future version of the same person swapped places every so often. I also wondered what the result would be if one of those swaps involved the remains of a corpse.* **Jumper,** *which was written in 2011, is one of the stories that combines both of the themes in this collection.*

Sunset

They knew this day would come once again. And, come once again, it had. Only it hadn't been expected for several millennia.

"What do you mean 'majestic'?" the female said.

"Maybe apocalyptic," the male replied.

She peers at him strangely.

They watched the sun as it set. It was the end of an era – but one that had lasted for a far shorter period than planned.

The sky that had, in long days past, been as blue as any they could ever remember, was now streaked yellow and orange. As the sun descended to the horizon, the flames danced in accompaniment.

"We have left it very late," he said, seeing the distant forests ablaze. "We should have returned to standard metabolism rates earlier."

"No matter," she countered. "Stabilisation will rectify any damage. Any species wiped out completely will be replaced from backup storage."

He nodded in agreement, though was still dismayed that they had not fully anticipated this event occurring so soon.

"We became complacent," he said. "We believed what the instruments told us. They were wrong – they missed the signs. This commenced more than ten thousand years ago – we should have been alerted."

"Yes," she said. "We will not make that mistake again. I will recalibrate them."

He moved to a bank of screens that showed different aspects of the planet from the satellites that, even still, remained in orbit.

"The icecaps retreat," he stated.

"They, too, will stabilise," she said.

"The sun won't."

"No," she said. "It won't."

They watched as, over a lengthy period of time, the burning day turned into night. But their night was hardly dark – the horizon was ringed with fire. Much of the land on this continent was now burning – they would need to replace almost all the wildlife in this hemisphere. They, at least, were safe as they watched from their control cabin. It was perched atop a thin support of metal that was located on a barren and sterile island of bare earth. It was their home.

"Destination," he said, indicating one of the stars above. It could just be seen through the smoke that threatened to blot out the view of the sky.

"Yes, I know," she said, her eyes momentarily fixing on that distant speck. "All readings indicate it is stable."

"That's what we thought about this one," he said.

"I told you. I will recalibrate the instruments."

He was silent for a while and then asked, "When is initiation?"

"Soon. Power is nearly at the minimum level required for successful departure. We dare not attempt initiation prior to that level."

"The world burns so much."

"It is true," she said.

"There will be little left."

"There will be enough."

Inwardly, he sighed, wondering if his companion had the capability to do the same. She, though, was evolved to be far more dispassionate than he.

"Initiation has commenced," she announced, finally.

He gazed out over the barren plain, adjusting the magnification of his vision to view the ashes that had once been verdant forests. Nothing fully alive could have survived there. It was still night but would not be for much longer. Another long day here would strip the land down to blackened bedrock.

Then his eyes swung up towards the heavens. The air was now far clearer than it had been when the last daylight had fallen here. He focussed on the star they'd designated 'Destination'. The engines kicked in and, as they did so, the star appeared to shimmer unnaturally for the merest sliver of time.

They were off, he thought, taking in the readouts on the screens. Their changing light patterns danced reflections onto the walls of the metal cabin.

"I have commenced hibernation mode," she stated.

He checked off the values being displayed before him. Already, temperatures across the globe were dropping. Soon, all would be in stasis.

"The world turns from fire to ice," he muttered.

She glanced at him, a quizzical expression passing across her features.

"Do you require recalibration?" she asked.

"No," he said quietly, noting the welcome increase in the distance between their world and the sun.

Much later they turned their eyes to the sky again. The sun's light was no longer enough to brighten the darkness of the land. Its disc was less than a fiftieth the size it had been. However, it should have been smaller still. But, if it had retained its previous dimensions, then there would not have been any need to flee.

"It will go nova soon," he stated.

"No," she said. "As you well know, it will merely expand into a red giant. It will take a while."

"Close enough."

She looked askance at him.

"Either way, it made no difference."

"Agreed," she said after a moment. "Revised estimates indicate that initial expansion is more than ninety-six percent imminent."

"Ah, and there it goes," he said, as the size of the disc suddenly increased.

They stood there watching as the expansion event unfolded. He checked the readings noting that they had attained enough acceleration to outrun it. He'd had his doubts but suspected that she hadn't. She was so much better at this than he.

As the planet's controlled rotation moved them out of direct view of the sun, he scanned the skies until Destination again became viewable.

"How long before we achieve orbit?" he asked. He already knew the answer to the last decimal point, but hadn't been able to resist the urge to voice the question

90

aloud.

She studied him again using the expression she had used before. "Twelve thousand, five hundred and sixty three original Earth years," she said, "as you well know."

"Yes," he said.

"I really will have to recalibrate you," she said.

"Yes," he said again.

It was going to be a long journey.

Sunset *was written in early 2020 in response to a Wattpad based monthly SF competition on the theme of a sunset. Much to my surprise, it won.*

The Fly Killer

I rage against the Barrier again. It is, as it always is, an impenetrable thing; a shield through which I cannot pass. It is my dread, my angst, but also my hope of a final exit.

It persists across the presumed termination of my previous existence, the host that was my life. I am now merely the unacknowledged traveller upon that life.

Girding all resource, channelling all resolve, I will myself to push hard against it. The Barrier's glare, white and uncompromising, induces nausea, though I am unable to be physically sick. I thrust my essence at it, into it, and experience the usual revulsion and terror. Like a cliff, white as chalk but as hard as granite, it relents not a millimetre.

In my failure I retreat back to somewhen less vivid, less stressful, less fearful.

I am again twelve or, I should say, the host upon whom I travel is twelve. I occupy his body, my body once, and I choose to feel all that he feels, think all that he thinks, emote all that he emotes. But the experience is merely second-hand. So I detach myself, and his feelings and emotions no longer impinge upon my own consciousness.

He goes about his life unknowing, never aware of me. At least I am certain that, before I first encountered the Barrier, I was never aware of being host to the traveller who is now me.

Through his eyes I view my surroundings. He sits upon the easy chair at my grandparent's home – its material worn and rendered plain through age. The room is a lounge – we called it a sitting room back then – though it is rarely used for such. It is for show, for Sunday best. It reeks of Sundays, closely packed as it is with furniture that is sombre in style and polished dark. The room is lit weakly by second-hand daylight from a window that faces north.

Despite the gloom of the room I know that, outside, the sun dances over a beckoning spring day that my host will not enjoy.

It is the year nineteen twenty-nine and we are dressed in his best attire, secluded away from the bustle that is mother and grandparents readying themselves for the weekly trip to church. I can feel his boredom as I have felt it so many times before. The air is punctuated every second by the grandfather clock ticking away my host's life. While it dominates the room it is not clamorous enough to drown out the buzz of a small but annoying fly.

Having witnessed it too many times before, I know what is about to transpire. Only once did I witness it for the first time but then it was just me as that twelve-year-old boy. Only then did I imagine I had the speed and accuracy to snuff out the fly's pathetic life when it landed upon the table beside me.

The fly lands as expected on the polished wood and, as flies do, occupies itself with rubbing its front legs together for a moment and passing them over its tiny head, cleaning its eyes. The host primes himself to smash his hand down upon it. I feel that thought and try to deter him from such pointlessness but I have no influence, so totally unaware is he of my presence within him. With no concern that the fly's blood will smear the crisply starched cuff of his white shirt, his arm falls. But the fly is too fast and, as usual, it ascends to the ceiling, circling three times as if mocking my host. Then it buzzes towards the window to repeatedly ping itself fruitlessly against the glass.

For a reason that fails to make itself clear to me I find this point in time compelling. I have visited it a countless number of times. The room, apart from the fly and clock, is tranquil and still. Although such stillness is at odds with my youthful host, it soothes away my loathing, fear and frustration with the Barrier. The room is dim and I am as alone as I can ever be.

After a while my host is collected by his family and the walk to church commences so, now being irreligious, I leave that time and travel back further.

Now my host is a five-week-old baby and I revel in the limitations that such a tender age experiences. My/his eyes have difficulty focussing upon their surroundings and stare wildly out of a high-barred cot. He is barely able to control the hands that grasp towards gaily-painted shapes that dangle close by.

I enjoy his frustration for a few moments and then plunge back even further.

Now I am in the womb, pulsating with my mother's heartbeat and heated by her body. I strain to make out sounds from outside. Swaddled and enveloped in the relaxing fluid, this is probably my second favourite time and place. I have come here many times since I became a separate mental entity from my host.

I am unable to determine how long it has been since that separation took place for I conjecture that I am no longer part of time itself. How can I objectively record my own perception of what I experience? I cannot control my host's physical body and have my own strange personal time outside of the linear form that my host experiences. I zip up and down his life experiencing moments again and again though, surprisingly, never meeting my current self on a return journey. Many times I have wondered how that can be, but have yet to formulate a reasonable explanation.

Yet I can never escape the physical confines of my host's body and life. Like an engine driver imprisoned in the cab of his train destined to travel a single, branchless track, there are no diversions from the monotony of the route upon which I am forced to ride.

I am dead. Of that I am sure.

Initially, I had been uncertain because the change from that life into this had been so unexpected. It was my experience that there was a point at which life stopped progressing in the normal way and the Barrier erected itself before me. The terror its sudden appearance generated had flung me backwards but, perplexingly, not in space. Instead, I had travelled backwards in time. It had taken me a while to learn to control that ability but, since then, I have had an unrecordable eternity of personal time.

So, I am dead. But I still have not determined how I died, though I am sure that my point of death lies either at or just beyond the Barrier. Stories of a person's whole life flashing before them at the point of death do not relate to my current existence. I had not expected to become a traveller upon that life, able to repeatedly return to any point from a few scant months after conception right up to the Barrier, but never outside those limits.

In truth, I hadn't expected anything upon death – just a cessation of everything that was me. Being, for the most part of my life, irreligious, I had not considered what came after. You were born, you grew up, you got old, you died. That was the end. Doctrines expounding reincarnation were alien to me. They exuded a wrongness that I was sure I would prove to myself upon my death by my immediate non-existence.

But, instead, I was bounced back and trapped in my previous life, possibly forever. I am convinced I will eventually go mad. In fact, I long for such madness if only to rid myself of the boredom.

With imaginary teeth gritted and filled with as much trepidation as before, I am back before the Barrier again. I am sure I am close to that point of death beyond which I can no longer exist, where I can finally rest. But, no matter how hard I strive for it, I am not actually able to perceive it – it is blocked and out of reach. I am as mystified by the Barrier now as I was when I first encountered it.

Despite the fear it induces, I have spent so much of my time at the Barrier itself that I have almost forgotten what comes in the moments preceding it. Restricted by my host's immutable path through life I retreat several minutes and observe what passes before my host's eyes. I catch a glimpse of my grandson. He shows me around his office; it is just a desk in a sea of desks in an open-plan hell. My host dislikes the surroundings, they are alien to him/me, but our grandson is proud of his place in the raging sea that is society, and so we nod and make appreciative remarks. He/I have travelled from the tranquillity of my home in the English Cotswolds, across the Atlantic to this noisy city as an early birthday treat from my grandson and his American wife. My host will be eighty-four in two days time, or would have been had he not presumably died.

A thought occurs. Although I presume his/my death is close beyond the Barrier, I still have no proof of this. What if my host can go beyond and I cannot?

No. That, I tell myself, is not reasonable. I am what my host becomes at the erection of the Barrier itself. He never experienced the other side because, when I was him, neither did I. So, what does lie beyond?

I have let time drift forward at the normal rate, which it does unless I deliberately move up or downstream, and the Barrier suddenly looms again. It is bright and fills everything with its stark impenetrability. As usual, I feel the terror rise up uncontrollably within myself but, as I fight it down, I twitch – I have just seen something I had never noticed before. Just before the brightness rears up I catch a glimpse of a woman's face out of the corner of my eye. I retreat a few seconds and watch her again. I cannot get her totally into focus for my host is not looking directly at her. I will his/my eyeballs to turn even minutely her way and concentrate, decelerating my passage of time so that the moment is replayed in slow motion.

Yes, I see something odd about her in that moment. Her expression changes in the last split second before the Barrier rises. Her eyes widen and she stares out the window. Just as the Barrier appears, her mouth begins to open as if in horror. Does she also see the terror that is the Barrier? Does she, at that point, also become a traveller upon the body that she once fully inhabited? For some reason that thought had never occurred to me – was the Barrier not just mine alone? Do others also encounter it? Including my grandson?

The precise tick, tick, tick of the clock soothes me. I have retreated to nineteen twenty-nine again. If I had been in possession of my own body then it would be shaking with the revelation of my discovery. The Barrier always scares me, terrifying me in a way that the dark barrier before my conception does not.

Yes, I have tried travelling back far beyond my birth but I find I slow down and my mind becomes cloudy. Possibly, I am relying upon the development of my host's facilities to sustain me. Beyond about six months prior to my birth I can hardly function. No matter how far I push myself back into the stupor of that early embryonic life, I find I just drift forward at time's normal rate until I become fully conscious of myself again. However, I am conscious right up to the Barrier. The dark barrier I can accept – the bright one I cannot. Although I have felt it, if 'felt' is the correct word, even though I have pushed against its impenetrableness, I still cannot conceive what it is and how it exists. Before the dark barrier there is nothing that was 'me' for I had not yet been conceived. Maybe that is also true of the bright one. It is possible that I cannot pass through it because, beyond, I do not exist?

So why do I insist that it is just that – a barrier? A barrier implies a division with something on either side. I am impelled to feel that there is more on the far side of my bright Barrier even though reason dictates that I can only find an empty death there.

There are no answers.

I turn my attention to my host who is annoyed by his church attire. Its stiffness rubs against his skin at cuff and collar. He is also annoyed by the sombreness pervading the room, along with the ticking of the clock. Mostly he is annoyed by the fly. I try to exert some influence, trying to quell his emotions and, maybe, I succeed.

Mentally, I chuckle a dry, silent laugh. Who am I kidding? I have no control over my host; have I not proved that time and again? He is watching the fly again as it lands, hand inaccurately poised for the kill. I know by how little he will miss and, playing a game I have ineffectually played so many times before, I try to divert the hand so that it hits the insect as he slams it down. Previously, when trying to influence him, I have concentrated with all of my mental ability. Now, casually resigned to the ridiculousness of the exercise; I know it is merely a hopeless game. So, I am surprised to see the room brighten slightly. Following this brightening, his hand diverts minutely from its usual course. Where it has spectacularly failed to make contact previously, my host's smallest finger now brushes against the insect. The fly cartwheels away upon a new path, one that's completely different to that which I've observed hundreds of times before.

I feel a moment of fear coupled with amazement. How is this possible? This life has been lived and all I do is travel its well-worn tracks as an observer. Did I really change it this time? Confused, I travel back and watch the scene again.

This time there is no increase in brightness. The hand falls, misses, and the fly takes off on its original path.

So what did I observe? Was I mistaken? Had I imagined it?

I retreat those few seconds again and try to divert the arm in the same carefree manner as before. But I find it hard to recapture the previous mood and fail in my endeavour. I try twice and then thrice before rushing back to the womb to console myself about my defeat. I meditate upon the problem and also to calm myself.

At length, a period of what, to me, may have been minutes, days or even years, I feel that maybe I have attained that mood again and I return to that moment. Now I exert the slightest influence upon my host's descending arm and, accompanied by a momentary increase of light, the hand brushes the fly again. It spins out of control in a manner completely different from before. I retreat and observe only, and the fly takes its original path.

Another attempt, the brightness and fear more intense, and the fly drops to the carpet, momentarily stunned before picking itself up to throw itself angrily at the window.

What is going on? What does it mean? The fear and brightness is that of the Barrier. What is it doing back here, more than seventy years before its appearance at my death?

I am elated, whilst simultaneously scared. I have spent an eternity travelling my previous life without affecting one iota of its solidly, rooted path. How long that has been I have little idea, though it seems like the time spent originally living as my host was nothing more than a mere fraction of that endured after the Barrier slammed itself across my path. But now, somehow, I have been able to make a change, a change that appears to be temporary but a change nonetheless; a change that hints of the Barrier itself.

Again, I push right back to the womb to think over the ramifications of my discovery. I choose a time when my mother is resting. She is in a bed shared with my father. I can hear his voice though I cannot make out the words. I concentrate upon the sounds my father makes but they are unintelligible. I conclude that the fault lies not with my hearing but due to the fact that the brain of my embryonic host is, at this stage, unable to understand what is being said. I long to see my father but, apart from photographs, I know this can never be. It is the summer of nineteen seventeen and, just before my birth, he is sent away from England to die pointlessly in the trenches in one of the battles against the Kaiser. He is destined never to see his child.

After a time I move forward, avoiding the moment of my birth near the middle of September. Only once did I try to follow my host through that traumatic event but it was too painful, too stressful and I had fled.

I halt at a moment when I suckle contentedly on my mother's milk and I consider an experiment. Previously, I have tried to influence my host at a later stage of his life, endeavouring unsuccessfully to wrest control over our shared body; I have never attempted it at a stage when he had less control. There is little I can achieve here except my own satisfaction that such things are possible.

Start small, someone once said.

So I try to gum down hard upon my mother's nipple, which is something my host never did. There is resistance but my host does not know what is happening. My mother emits a small, barely audible gasp as she feels the pressure. I try again and she pulls my host away from her chest and I stare into her frowning eyes with my own. Her face shines with a fearsome, bright light that she obviously cannot detect. The effect fades quickly and the track of my life rejoins its original route as she replaces me to her chest.

But that event is totally new. It never happened. I retrace a minute and let events unfold again without interference. This time the sequence plays out as it was meant to be and I stay attached, feeding.

So I return to the Barrier, to observe the horrified woman again and wonder what she sees. Her expression becomes clearer as I manage to influence my host's vision to focus more upon her face. I try to hold that moment, concentrate upon it as the Barrier rises from wherever it comes. With the same calmness of mind that enabled me to swat the fly and pain my mother, I try to hold back the Barrier so that I can observe the split second after its brightness normally obscures everything. Moments that, in real time, take no more than a second are, to my perception, elongated into minutes as I drive myself to attain that perfect detached serenity.

Then the woman shouts, "Jesu-"

This I never heard before, previously her shout had been cut off by the Barrier. Unbelievably, I have gained about half a second. I retreat and watch it again. The Barrier cuts off the end of her exclamation and I have to gently impose a greater level of serenity upon myself, to plunge down to deeper, calmer levels to push it further. After several attempts I know that she cries, "Jesus Christ."

I am sure she says more but I feel exhausted, drained but, oh, so elated. I have won a small battle.

I return to the womb to recuperate and luxuriate in its safety. Here, more than eighty decades before the Barrier, I can rebuild myself for a new attack. I do not sleep. I have not slept since first encountering the Barrier, which becomes interesting as it means I can observe my host's dreams in detail. I allow something approaching a month of real time to slowly drift forward at its own pace before determining I am fully recharged. In that time I have practiced my meditations, honed my burgeoning skills. In that time I have regained a purpose.

Also, I have begun to admit to myself that my previous beliefs may have been wrong. The state of mind that I had found myself attaining during my successful attempts at swatting the fly and fighting the Barrier have possibly hinted at a continuation of some sort. I no longer seek to pass the Barrier for its offer of extinction but, instead, for the scant promise of something that goes on. I am not wholly convinced that what could remain to go on would fully be myself but, if only a part of my essence manages to pass over to another state, then I shall be content. This, then, is my new purpose.

Still, the fear that the Barrier instils within me is strong. I have been fighting that fear for so long now that I do it almost naturally. Then another thought overloads me – what if I give in to that fear totally? Embrace it instead of fighting it? Would that allow me to achieve my objective?

It is, I conclude, worth trying.

My contemplation over, I start to skim forward. On my journey something makes me stop off at a few significant points of my ordinary life: my first sexual experience with a girl; my wedding to Jessica; the births of our son and daughter, their weddings and the subsequent production of their offspring; the loss of Jessica to cancer at only fifty-nine; and the landing at Kennedy Airport as I begin my trip in America. But, before I go forward to the Barrier itself, I suddenly plunge backwards to that quiet Sunday.

The clock ticks and the fly buzzes, and the scene plays itself out yet again. My host raises his arm ready for the fly to land, which it eventually does, and I feel my host's arm tense as he readies it. I slow my passage forward so that I experience time at about a quarter speed. As the arm starts to descend I elevate myself into my new state of fear-accepting serenity and the room about me glows with the unnatural brightness. I gently will the arm sideways by a mere inch. My host tries to resist my efforts but I calmly fight back and gain ground. The bright fear washes over and through me, but its sting is now welcome.

With my host's hand a mere five inches above the fly the insect realises the danger but it no longer has the same wide avenue of escape. The hand connects with it and crushes the life from its tiny, frail body and a spurt of juice taints the cuff of the crisp, white shirt. He/I smile and I experience his brand new thoughts that, should the stain be noticed, the scolding that was sure to follow will have been worth the thrill and satisfaction of the kill.

I retreat a few minutes and watch the scene again and again. Amazingly, the time-stream, the track, or whatever it can be called, has locked itself onto this new sequence of events. Without any further input from myself, the fly's life is now extinguished every time. I have permanently changed a small part of my host's life. I feel no remorse for the death of the fly. It has died to give me new hope, to confirm my new purpose.

What I wonder, could have happened to the previous set of events? Could I influence the fall of the arm so that it would again miss its target? For a moment I entertain the possibility, but then realise I have a bigger challenge and fly forwards to the Barrier.

When I arrive I find that I can observe right up to the end of the woman voicing, "Jesus," and I have to calmly fight again for the rest of her exclamation. This I do and achieve another full second of revelation. As the woman speaks I find my host beginning to turn his head in order to observe what has caused her distress. His view passes over my grandson and I note that his face, too, is turning in the same direction as the woman's. My grandson's face has also begun to take on an expression of horror but, as yet, my host has not turned far enough. What can they be seeing? They must be looking out of the window. What could they possibly see from this high building?

Serenely, I gather my strength and push ahead, determined this time to see if I can observe what causes the rise of the Barrier.

For a time that's impossible to measure, I drive my mental state deeper and calmer. The fear that previously caused me to shrink away now envelopes me and, at last, I fully accept it. And, as I do so, I slowly become aware of a change in the Barrier. No longer is it impervious to my efforts. Its burning heat is reduced and it is less solid. It is now malleable to my thrust and I become enclosed within it. As we merge it is like I am made of Barrier stuff myself. The fear with which it had previously glowed is now merely a sparkle that is drowned in the glow from myself. It is now I that burn with brightness and it is the turn of the Barrier to cringe in fear at its new opponent.

Suddenly, the Barrier's brightness is no longer before me and, ahead of me, is a soft darkness that hardly reflects the glow behind. My own burning has also been extinguished, its job accomplished. I glance past-wards to see the Barrier still standing and realise that I am seeing it from the other side. It is pale and translucent, merely a glass wall through which I can see. I become aware that I am also no longer tethered to my host. The track upon which I have ridden for an eternity no longer anchors me.

I am free of my prison.

Before me, in the darkness, a new spark of beckoning light appears and its call promises continuation of a sort. Now I realise that I have fully conquered fear and have a complete belief in a new future.

I am about to accept my new journey when I decide to take one last glance behind me. In the brightness, which is no longer a Barrier, it takes me a moment to understand what I am viewing. My vision, no longer restrained by the limitations of human eyes, can simultaneously capture the events that have occurred over the final few seconds. It is as if they are set in overlapping frames of a film. In those scant moments of freeze-frame I see my host's body, along with my grandson's, the woman and everyone else in that office, instantly char, burn and evaporate in a horrifyingly bright explosion that is the Barrier.

No longer restricted by my host's body, I see the reason for their expressions. And before answering the call of my new future I gasp at that last terrible scene.

Will I ever be able to erase the image of an aeroplane plunging into the heart of the building?

Written in 2003 The Fly Killer *was the second attempt at using an idea of someone moving up and down their own timeline almost at will. The first, penned earlier in 2003, had been a "first contact" type of story where alien ambassadors, who also possessed this ability, had been dispatched to Earth to apparently welcome us into some sort of Galactic Federation. However, I was never satisfied with the way that particular story turned out, so had reused the idea a short while later.*

Blue Pearls

"Please avert your eyes now."

The announcement over the trawler's tannoy is unnecessary. We all know what time the damn thing is due to be dropped. Seething with anger, and at the throbbing pain in my thumb, I glance at my watch. The light from the setting sun reflects off its face as I angle it to view the hands. Two minutes. Surely, we're still far too close.

But, we are expendable. Sacrificial lambs along with all the real lambs that had to be left behind and are scheduled to die today. Those that still survive, that is, which is probably coming closer to zero with each passing second.

The fire within me grows as I think about my home and my flocks, but I keep my eyes towards the west; where the old enemy wait.

If nothing else, this will at least put an end to their claims upon us.

The trawler cuts through the waters of the South Atlantic ploughing towards Puerto Santa Cruz. The sky, blue and innocent with hardly a cloud, belies the danger that now rides high above us, far out of sight. Beside the ship, the sea echoes the sky, the swell is subdued, faking the promise that all is well.

The ship stinks of fish – or squid probably. But I am a shepherd, not a fisherman – the stink of the sea is all the same to me. This isn't my element. Here I am, packed along with a hundred others – crying children, whimpering mothers, furrowed-faced fathers – all of us racing far too slowly for our lives. Somewhere on this boat are the rest of my family: my younger sister and parents. The dogs, even Jess, had to be abandoned.

Facing away from home, I watch the sea, the shallow rise and fall of calm, hoping that we have truly escaped. Someone starts a countdown from thirty as my eyes skim the waves. As the count reaches twenty-two I see it: glistening in the sunlight, a large fish, probably a tuna, floating at the surface. Exactly where it shouldn't have been. It flaps feebly on its side. My rage turns to fear. It's all been a waste of time.

I shout and point at the fish as the count drops to fifteen. Those around me groan. Dotted along the side of the fish are small blue spheres, glinting in the sun like so many pearls. The blue is neither that of the sea nor of the sky. Intense and unnatural, this blue is wrong on so many levels.

More surface around the fish, and then dozens appear. One by one they close and latch onto the fish, which is now limp.

There's a flash from behind me, accompanied by screams and shouting. Damn, the count had only reached six. I screw my eyes shut and grind my teeth together.

Gone. All gone. Our home, the flocks and all that I had ever known. Wiped from the face of the Earth and, for what?

The rage inside me explodes. I scream at no one in particular, "Too late, you bloody fools. They've already escaped."

But, I was as much a fool as those who had just destroyed our home. I was the one who had discovered them. Had it really been only six days ago? Even if I knew then what I know now, could I have made any difference?

Like my father before me, I had tended the Corriedales all my life. Bred them, reared them, sheared them, sold them, eaten them. They were the hub about which our family lived and worked. Not that I had gone far along life's road. At twenty-five, I thought I still had far more years ahead of me than behind.

I was up in the hills with Jessie, one of our dogs. The flock, though it ranged over a wide area, mostly stayed grouped together. Jessie was there to help me round them up for a trip back to the sheds for shearing. I'd started early, well before sunrise, and driven most of the way up on the quad bike before dismounting to enjoy the crispness of the morning air. It was a rare day when it wasn't crisp.

With a couple of whistles and a hand gesture, I'd sent Jess off to tackle a few sheep that had strayed from the others. While she was gone I spotted it. The streak that lit up the pre-dawn sky was no normal meteor. I'd seen shooting stars many times and knew they were particles of comet dust grazing the upper reaches of the atmosphere. This was different. The hairs on my neck stood to attention seconds before I heard the sound of it passing close overhead. Then the hills shook, followed barely a second later by a noise like thunder, only it wasn't.

"Damn, a meteorite, an actual meteorite," I said to the sheep around me, many of which were now running downhill, away from where it had landed. That didn't last long, and the exodus ground to a halt once they perceived they were in no immediate danger.

I don't know how long I stood there, just staring at the point of light where the meteorite had come to ground. But, once the glow died down I instructed Jessie to remain with the sheep and then I was off. I ran towards where I'd last seen the light, the sheep forgotten for once.

It took me about fifteen minutes to reach the crater. Just before it there were scorch marks along the ground. I approached cautiously and peered over the rim as the sun breached the horizon, its rays painting the normal brown and sparse green vegetation of the island with a ruddy tint.

The crater, while it was more than twice my height in width, was no more than a disappointing three feet or so in depth. Half buried near its centre there were a couple of lumps of rock, each glowing a dull red. They resembled nothing more than an egg cracked into two uneven pieces. Steam rose idly from each half – though not enough to suggest it might be dangerous. And that in itself was strange. Surely something that small should have completely burned up in the atmosphere. Then again, what did I know? I was no expert on these things.

Then a movement near the steaming rocks caught my eye. A tiny object, like a snail shell moved with deliberation up the slope of the crater towards me. I stepped closer. It was deep blue, an intense shade that almost hurt the eyes. It was combined with a texture that glistened like pearl which, despite the darkness within the crater, gave the impression it was emitting its own light. Just over a couple of inches across and almost spherical, it was mottled with bulges that were unevenly distributed around the body, like a badly made golf ball in reverse. It rolled slowly up the incline leaving no clue as to how it was achieving this. I reached out, my hand hesitating above it in case it was too hot to touch. I couldn't detect any and picked it up. It was dry and warm on the palm of my hand, but not excessively so. I held it up between forefinger and thumb to get a better look. The bulges squirmed under my touch in a manner that made me feel nauseous, and I had to fight the urge to drop it.

Then, a couple of the larger bulges stuck out like a beak. I was about to drop it when it twisted position and nipped into the tip of my thumb, completely removing a chunk of flesh, leaving a notch that immediately oozed blood.

I screeched and dropped it, swearing profusely. The damned thing rolled back towards the meteorite rocks as I stared at the gash that started to ooze. Seeing the blood I pushed my thumb into my mouth. Sucking seemed to reduce the flow of blood, though the throbbing that replaced it promised pain for days to come. As I sucked, my tongue followed the contours of the removed flesh. I pulled it from my mouth and gasped at the damage – it had gone almost down to the bone.

My eyes caught more movement. The thing that had bitten me was crawling back up the crater slope, and coming straight towards me. And it wasn't the only one – there were seven or eight of the things, all inching directly towards where I stood. I heard a scraping sound – one of the damned things was trying to bite into the leather of my boot. I flicked it off with the toe of the other boot before bringing my heel right down on top of it, crushing it to pulp.

Then, in a rage, I ran around stamping on as many of the things as I could, leaving a trail of slimy marks in the broken ground. The rising sun picked out more of the things, some of which had already reached the crater rim and were disappearing from view.

After completing a circuit of the crater I turned my attention to the escapees. I managed to crush twenty or so that were making their way across the grass but I had no idea how many I might have missed. I returned to the crater and gasped. The sticky patches of crushed gunk were no longer static. They were oozing across the ground and regrouping. Open mouthed, I watched one patch of slime grow. Once it had reached about six inches across, an outer skin formed over it, which divided several times. A minute later about thirty new tiny snail things started crawling towards me. And the other patches were doing the same. More than twenty snail things had merged into five patches of mush and now more than a hundred tiny versions of the originals were hunting me down.

I backed away, treading on another bunch that had come up from behind me. I turned and ran, charging back down the hill. With a call to Jessie, I leapt on the quad bike and gunned it home as fast as I could.

Of course, no one believed my story once I'd reached home. My sister said I'd probably fallen asleep and got bitten by a Giant Petrol. But, later that afternoon, after a trip to the doctor in Port Stanley to examine my thumb, one of our close neighbours – they only lived a couple of miles away – paid us a visit. Like us, George and his family's lives revolved around their sheep. He was currently grazing his on the other side of the hill from our flock.

As he leapt from his Land Rover, George's eyes were full of panic and it didn't take long to find out why. In the trailer behind the vehicle lay two of his flock – both dead and chewed almost to the bone.

"I tried to get them off," he cried. "But they grew back."

All of us – George, myself, my sister, Mum and Dad – stared at the writhing corpses. The glistening blue forms moved slowly and deliberately over them, devouring anything they could, be it flesh, bone or wool.

"Oh my God," my sister said. "You weren't joking."

A few of the things dropped off the trailer and rolled towards us. My Dad stomped on one.

"Don't," I shouted. "They just turn into more."

"You can't kill the bastards," George whispered, the shock pasting his face white. We all watched as the crushed creature reconstituted itself not back as one, but as five.

"I bet they won't be able to stand a bit of heat," my Dad said, grinning humourlessly, and went to retrieve the cutting torch.

He fired it up and aimed the flame at two of the larger blue pearl things on the ground.

"Hah," he said, "look – burnt to a crisp."

Indeed, the two creatures were no longer blue and, possibly more important, no longer moving. They and a few inches of the ground around them were black.

"We should torch those sheep to kill the rest," Dad said, talking to George. They unhitched the trailer and pushed it away from the Land Rover.

"Wait," my sister said, pointing to the charred mess on the ground. "They're fizzing."

There was a sound like two pieces of popcorn popping as the creatures exploded, splattering tiny, bright-blue pellets up to five feet away from the blackened circle. Each one immediately sought out something live – grass in this case – and started eating.

As we backed away, George's radio went off.

"Yes," he said. "Oh, my God. Get out of there. Quickly."

We stared at George as he cut the connection.

"Lizzie – she said they're all over the house. I've got to go and get her."

We weren't the first to report them to the authorities.

Someone driving along the Darwin Road had seen an injured sheep and taken photos of the things crawling through its wool.

Within forty eight hours the damned things were as far north as Green Patch, south to Bluff Cove and some had been seen on the outskirts of Stanley itself. They had been observed eating anything, grass, sheep, birds – even the plastic waste pollution washed up on beaches. As they ate, they grew and once they were around four inches across, they split into a hundred new ones the size of grains of rice. The wind carried the tiny ones off and on landing they just carried on eating.

By the time the order to evacuate came over the radio, we had already abandoned the farm. By nightfall on the second day, the land around it had been eaten down to the bare soil. If any of the flock remained then they had scattered far beyond our capability to locate them. Piling the four-by-four high with essentials, we'd taken flight before sunrise the next morning and headed west and then south along the Darwin Road. In the dark, the hills were like a galaxy of stars, but stars in the sky never shone with such an intense blue.

Then we found we were carrying the damned things with us. Those blue snails crushed by our tyres as we escaped had set up small colonies within the wheel arches. On the radio we'd heard a rumour that car de-icer would slow them down, and we had stop every so often to spray under the arches to remove the unwelcome passengers. It was only a temporary respite and, while the stops to rid ourselves of the things were required less often, that didn't halt the unrelenting appetite of the creatures. We'd lost half the dogs to them before we'd shaken the damn things off.

Goose Green, once we'd reached it was almost free of the things. However, the news that more were heading south towards the narrow ridge that connected the north and south parts of the island, meant that nowhere on the east island was safe.

Like many, we spent the fourth day getting across to Port Howard on the west island, hoping that by doing so, we could escape the creatures.

We were wrong. Maybe it was the wind, maybe they had been brought across accidentally – however they had come was no longer important.

And then we learned of how the authorities, for once quick to respond to such an emergency, were going to deal with it.

A hand rests on my arm.

"It's all over, isn't it?" my sister says. I put my arm around her as she breaks down and sobs.

But, suddenly, a wind from nowhere transforms the calm, tipping the ship alarmingly to one side. My sister and I grasp at each other, and I hold her close as we fight to retain our footing. I search around for Mum and Dad but they are nowhere in sight. There are more screams and at least one splash. I can't resist a glance back and catch a glimpse of the mushroom cloud. My breath catches in my throat. So high, and far too close. The captain struggles to retain control but the man-made storm is now upon us and it's obviously a battle to keep the prow pointing westward.

But it's all in vain. We are tainted. Beside us, the churning water shows more floating fish and all have passengers of their own. Only the fish are dead; the blue pearls, seemingly unaware of the maelstrom erupting in the air above them, just carry on eating.

At least they haven't managed to board the ship – they haven't developed a taste for bare metal… yet. How long would it be before they would?

Towards the west, Puerto Santa Cruz is over three hundred miles away. Even I know that trawlers like this have a top speed of no more than around ten knots – barely twelve miles an hour. Just how long will it take to reach the coast? Do we have enough fuel?

As I gaze out across the sea, the fall of dusk and the shadow of the mushroom cloud darkens the waves. And, that darkness only makes the blue pearls shine brighter as they continue to devour everything they can. After a while there are far less fish and too many blue pearls, and they are as far ahead of us as they are behind.

As I hold my sister in my arms, fear dominates my thoughts. Even if we ever manage to achieve landfall, I dread to imagine what will await us there.

This was one of the few stories I have ever written that originated from a dream. In the dream I had only imagined the **Blue Pearls** *and how they couldn't be killed but would multiply and grow. The story was written within a few days of the dream in 2017.*

Too Complicated

ZORG stood preening himself in front of the mirror. He was particularly impressed with the bushiness of his eyebrows and the luxuriousness of his beard. He turned his head, first this way and then that, so that the fine white hairs sparkled with ethereal light. No wonder he had impressed the humans so many times back in the old days.

He considered taking another trip down there but sighed. He knew there would always be a certain number of the damned sods trying to disprove his existence even while he stood in full view of them waving his arms. It hadn't been like that with the Ancient Greeks who knew him as Zeus or the Norsemen who called him Odin. Okay, so the Egyptians had been a funny bunch insisting that he rode around with his chariot on fire, but at least they hadn't questioned his omnipotence. He chuckled as he remembered another lot. Oh yes, forty years in a desert and no one asking directions – a complete hoot.

But, as for the current incumbents… bloody atheists.

There was a commotion outside.

"Dad, Dad."

His son, TJ, hammer in one hand and something else in the other, ran in breathlessly.

"What in Hades?"

"Look at this," TJ said. Like ZORG he was following the current fad of constructing his moniker from the initials of his past names – not as impressive as ZORG but TJ still had a good ring to it – the T stood for Thor. Originally, he'd used his Buddha initial until someone pointed out that BJ probably wasn't such a good idea.

TJ dropped his hammer and unrolled the thing he was carrying. Text and images appeared on it – they swum as ZORG stared at them.

"What the buggery is it? Hold the blasted thing still," he growled.

"Newspaper," TJ explained, holding up the thin plastic sheet in front of his father.

"Paper? This isn't paper."

"Just focus here on the headline area first. Apparently it scans your face to see where you're looking and then magnifies that bit so you read it. Bloody clever. Works by touch, too."

"Too damned complicated. What's wrong with stone tablets? Good enough in my day. Humans – they mess with everything they shouldn't — that's always been our job."

"There, that bit." TJ pointed at a headline, which expanded so that the entire article filled the sheet. Now the display was unmoving, apart from the date and time in the top right corner, which showed 'May 12, 2438 – 14:07:06'.

The headline ran: Jupiter's Moons Didn't Exist Before 1610 – Proof!

ZORG read a couple of paragraphs and then threw the newspaper to his feet where it rolled itself back up into a thin tube.

"Who's this Professor Qwertyuiop? One of ours? It's not SLIR or whatever he's calling himself these days, is it?" ZORG stormed.

"No, Dad, just a normal human. Clever one, though. Invented a time machine, put it in his air car and went back to visit that Italian bloke, Galileo."

"WHAT? Time machine? Who the hell allowed that?"

"Um, well… you did actually… when you approved the 'splitting the atom' change a few centuries back. Time travel was just a consequence of all that quantum stuff coming into being."

"Pah – trying to keep ahead of the little sods is getting harder and harder. Time was when all you had to do was make sure the sun rose in the morning and the moon went round once a month. It's the fault of that bloody brother of yours. 'Keep one step ahead of the bastards. Always make things just a bit more complicated than they can understand,' he'd chant. Now look where it's got us."

"Yeah, yeah, Dad," TJ replied. He'd heard this rant many times before. Anyway, back then ZORG had positively encouraged SLIR to 'complicate things up' for humankind.

And SLIR (Satan, Lucifer, Iblis, Rahu – his brother really hadn't got the hang of it) went about it with no little relish. He'd rebuilt the planets — converting them from small blobs stuck on crystal spheres spinning around a flat Earth into giant lumps of free-floating matter millions of miles away.

Not bad for an afternoon's work.

Later on SLIR reworked the stars, changing them from glowing lights embedded in another crystal sphere into huge fiery, nuclear globes. Building billions of light years worth of expanding space took him the best part of a week — they even had to relocate bits of the underworld to fit that lot in.

Not that SLIR didn't like adding his own touches to things — ZORG was well pissed off when he discovered the dinosaur skeleton with the gold fillings. Good job the humans didn't get wind of it first – unlike that sea monster SLIR created and stashed in a lake somewhere in northern Europe a few hundred years ago.

"That bloody Galileo," ZORG was fuming. "He was a trouble maker from the start. Had an idea to smite him at the time. You talked me out of it, I seem to remember."

TJ grinned and shrugged. He didn't have his Dad's penchant for smiting. In fact he had a bit of a soft spot for the humans – despite them once nailing him to a tree when he'd taken an extended holiday down there.

"So, what are you going to do about that infernal professor?" ZORG demanded.

"Well, we can't stop him from going back to 1610 'cause he's already done that and it's been documented by the humans. Maybe we can discredit him or something."

"Discredit him — DISCREDIT HIM! Smear the little shit across several mountain ranges as a lesson to the rest of the 'em, more like."

"Er, yes, Dad."

ZORG noticed the expression on TJ's face and relented. "Okay, okay. Just make sure he doesn't find out about anything else. Bump him off — quietly or noisily — don't care which, and I don't care how you do it. Make it look like an accident if you must."

"Right."

***

TJ ran off to find SLIR and located him sitting under an apple tree in a rarely used garden. He was disguised as a small girl and feeding nails to a unicorn. He looked up as TJ arrived.

"How'd he take it?" he said, reverting to his normal appearance, which caused the unicorn to take fright and gallop away.

"Usual. Wants us to fix it."

"What a surprise. Say — what do you think of BAM?"

"Eh?"

"Be, Ay, Em – BAM – from Beelzebub, Azazel and Mephistopheles."

"Oh. I see, yeah. Probably better than SLIR."

"Right. Let it be known that from this day forwards I shall be known as..."

"Yeah, whatever. Back to the point."

"Oh, right, the time travelling professor. Might be a bit difficult."

"Why?"

"He's left the twenty-fifth century again. Not sure where or when he's gone."

"Oh, Jees."

"Don't take your own name in vain," SLIR/BAM mocked. "Did Dad give us permission to time travel?"

"Not in so many words – did say he didn't care how we bumped him off, though."

"Good enough for me. Let's go. You don't like BAM, do you?"

***

"There he is," whispered SPOD (ex SLIR/BAM – SPOD = Shaitan + Pan + Orcus + Diabolus). He and TJ were watching the professor from the concealment of a tree — slightly pointless, as they were cloaked and therefore undetectable to human ears and eyes. Professor Qwertyuiop was standing on a low cliff top with his eye to a complex device that was trained upon the distant shore.

"Neat car," TJ added, spying the professor's silver air car parked a few yards further along the cliff. Its retractable roof, half open, billowed slightly in the warm breeze.

"It's no De Lorean, though."

"What?"

"Nothing."

"What's he looking at?" TJ asked. "And that thing he's looking through — is that a telescope or something else?"

"Search me. Where and when are we anyway?"

"Greek island. Dunno which one. The prof seems to be looking at another island."

They'd tracked the tachyon trail from his airborne time machine back into the past but neglected to check on the date. Still, returning to the present was no problem to deities of their calibre.

SPOD scratched at his beard thoughtfully. "You reckon we could push him off this cliff?"

"Hmm. Not very high, is it? He'd probably survive the fall."

Suddenly, without noise or warning, the horizon shifted.

"Whoa. What the hell was that?" TJ shouted. He was confused — there had been no roar as the land moved, something he would have expected from an earthquake. Additionally, the ocean remained suspiciously calm. But the view had changed — the horizon was distinctly lower and the other island was now barely visible.

"Ah, I see," SPOD nodded as the professor packed his telescope away and returned to his car. "I know exactly when we are."

TJ raised an eyebrow.

"Obvious. It's the day I converted the world from flat to round."

TJ noticed the air car lifting into the sky. "I suppose we'd better stop him going back to the future with more proof. You want to zap him or shall I?"

The car swivelled in the air and then popped out of existence.

"Bugger, too late."

Following the tachyon trail they were perplexed when, instead of jumping forwards to the twenty-fifth century, it moved backwards a couple of hours and then shot off westward towards the Atlantic. They caught up with him at the edge of the still-flat Earth but, as they approached the car, the Professor disappeared again.

"Sod it," SPOD moaned. "Must've seen us. Damn, we forgot to turn on our cloaking devices. Pity. We really could have pushed him over the edge here."

Below them the waters of the Atlantic Ocean crashed over the edge of the Earth to hurtle into the black depths below.

"No way would his air car have worked in all that salty spray," SPOD chuckled. "Would have left no trace, either."

"Where does all the water go?" TJ asked. He'd never thought about it before. SPOD had always been the one interested in the technical details.

"Ask Dad. His great omnipotence put it all together in less than a week on a bet – before your time that was. I junked it all and started again when I did the conversion." SPOD scratched his head. "I think the water gets squirted out the top of mountains as clouds or something like that. Always thought my idea of evaporation was much neater."

They watched the water for a few more minutes. Here, they could make out the crystal spheres that enclosed the Earth. Below, out of the sunlight, the stars stuck to the outer crystal were glowing in a distinctly unnatural manner.

"A right bodge job, wasn't it?" SPOD murmured. "All made out of four elements, too."

"Elephants?"

Suddenly the scenery jumped again and the cascade was replaced by normal ocean. To the west they could see a new continent.

"Bugger and double bugger. We shouldn't have waited," SPOD said.

TJ sighed. "I've lost the trace. Your reconstruction has wiped it out."

"That's right, blame me. Hold on, I'm picking something up a few thousand years hence."

They leapt forward to Europe. It was night.

"Isn't this where he first appeared?" TJ said, as they followed the tachyon trail across the countryside. "Look, this is Italy. Pizza and leaning towers and all that. And bloody Romans," he added with a shudder.

"Don't think pizzas and the Roman Empire were synonymous…"

"Whatever… aha." TJ swooped down. "There he is – got that telescope thing out again, pointing into the air this time."

They landed on the side of the hill above their prey and silently drifted down until they were a few yards away from the professor.

"Yep," SPOD said, "but this is his first trip back – where he's discovering that Dad only put the moons around Jupiter to give Galileo something to think about. That red spot on Jupiter was my suggestion – though I actually wanted to put it on Galileo's eyelid instead just to make it hard for him to look into his telescope. Dad got the wrong end of the stick – or telescope in this case."

"Pity we can't bump him off here, then."

"Nope. The Cause and Effect department will get in a right huff if we stop him from returning home the first time. We've got to cut him off before he returns home for the second time."

"Unless he has already."

SPOD sighed. "Don't confuse me any more than I already am…"

"So where's he gone now?"

***

"Ah, there you are," said the newly renamed SCAB (Supay + Chernobog + Akuma + Belial), three (relative) days later. "I think I've finally found him. Follow me."

"Where are we going?"

"Ancient Turkey and about a hundred and fifty years Before You."

As they travelled back through time SCAB said, "Where have you been, by the way, you haven't exactly been on the job, have you?"

"Yes I have. I went back to see if the prof had come to my execution."

"And had he?"

"Didn't see him."

"Hmm, you were probably too busy to notice."

"It was a very difficult time for me," TJ sniffed.

"Bloody disaster, more like. Anyway, whose idea was it to do the reincarnation act?"

"I wanted to put on a show."

"Rabbits out of hats would have been good enough for that lot."

"Well, you didn't exactly help beforehand when you tried to talk me out of it in the desert."

"We needed a fourth for Bridge and you had promised…"

They emerged into bright sunshine.

"There he is."

SCAB pointed into the distance. The professor was sitting in his air car talking to someone.

"Who's that?" TJ asked.

"Hipparchus. He's the one who figured out I moved the Earth from the centre of the solar system and plonked the sun there instead."

"He looks a bit twitchy," TJ said as the professor nervously peered around before his gaze stopped to rest upon them.

"Damn," SCAB said, "I keep forgetting to turn on the invisibility cloak thingy."

The car zipped into the air and disappeared.

***

"WHAT? Still alive?" ZORG thundered.

"Yeah, but it's not easy," TJ said, ignoring the lightning sparking from his father's fingertips that threatened to zap SCAB's toes. "He's a wily sod and he's on to us. He keeps himself around others so we can't intervene without giving ourselves away or zap him from a distance without hitting others which might screw up history."

"Too bloody soft, the pair of you."

"We tried to drop a branch on him when he went to see Newton," SCAB intervened, "but TJ only managed to disturb a few apples. Missed the Prof completely."

"A few apples?" ZORG's face turned a deep crimson, and both TJ and SCAB took a step backwards. This was getting serious. "Right, you useless sods. I'll show you how it should be done."

ZORG drew himself up to his full height. "Where is he now?"

"Um. Mid-twentieth century — in the New World. Not sure what he's after this time," TJ offered.

"Here's the tachyon trace," SCAB said, conjuring up a map and timeline vision.

ZORG took one look and then disappeared. TJ and SCAB glanced at each other, shrugged and followed.

ZORG's turbulent time-wake deposited them in the desert scrub of New Mexico. They spotted their father some yards away staring up into the sky.

"Found your bloody professor," ZORG growled, his eyes tracking a small dot arcing across the sky and coming closer. "He's alone and there's no potential witnesses around here."

"What are you going to do when he lands?"

"Lands? Bugger that. Time for a bit of smiting..."

ZORG raised his hands and a beam of energy crackled skyward to zap the descending craft. It shattered into a cloud of silvery pieces, the fragments spiralling towards the ground.

"Right, you bloody amateurs. That's how it should be done."

"Won't the remains of the air car cause temporal problems?" TJ questioned.

"Who cares. At least the troublesome little bastard's dead," ZORG said before

120

ascending to the heavens.

TJ shook his head as the remains of the air car settled on the desert.

"Don't worry," SCAB said as the two of them started to fade from view, "I'll start a rumour that it was just a weather balloon or something. I mean, it's only 1947 — humans of this period really are quite dumb. They'll believe anything."

Too Complicated *was a 2007 rewrite of an earlier, and more serious, version from 2004 that hadn't been completed as it was from the perspective of the occupant of the time travelling vehicle. However, given that the character wouldn't survive and that his opponents were originally going to be extra-terrestrial, the ending wouldn't have worked. The Tom Holt influences of this rewrite are rather obvious.*

Wisdom of the Ancients

"Oh look, mother," the daughter said. "What is it?"

The mother drew nearer to see what the daughter had discovered. They had been travelling across the land for the past two thousand years, the daughter marvelling at all the sights the mother pointed out. The mother adjusted her vision to view the tiny thing over which her daughter towered.

"Ah, be careful, daughter. It is very fragile and rare. It is called old life. Let it see the light."

"What is it doing?"

"It is growing in the way that only old life could. Form yourself a magnifier and observe the particles from which it is constructed."

The daughter did so taking only a dozen cycles of the passing sun to construct the device from transparent parts of her body. At each passing of the sun overhead the old life grew taller, swaying from side to side as it followed the passage of the light above.

"I think it is what the ancients called çəmənli, or herbe, or maybe grass for they had so many tongues and I have only had a chance to explore a few over the past twelve million years."

"It is very green now. Why is it so rare?"

"The world is very changed from what it was, daughter. Old life like this is not built for the world as it is now."

"Why not?"

"The ancients changed it so that it would be fit for us. They changed the air and filled the world with the long-lasting materials like the plastics from which we construct ourselves. They were very wise and selfless for they created a world in which only new life such as ourselves could flourish."

"Oh look again, mother. There are new things growing at the top of the green parts."

The mother observed for another couple of weeks and then searched through the nano-particles from which her memories were constructed. She altered a few pathways within her bulk to correlate the information with data derived originally from ancient resources.

"They are, I believe, called seeds," she said finally. "One of the manners by which old life propagated itself. Not very efficient as observation of these show they are sterile for they require a process called pollination in order to fulfil their purpose."

"Oh, the green is beginning to fade," the daughter said with a mournful tone to her utterance. Around them the daylight grew dimmer and the temperature fell.

"Indeed. Old life is extremely brief. From what we can determine, the ancients themselves had lifespans that were measured in only tens of years. It is no wonder they sought to restructure the world as they did."

The old life withered and died.

"Can we go back to the sea?"

"Yes, daughter. It is time for you to become an adult, increasing your bulk from the plastics the ancients so thoughtfully filled it with."

"The ancients were wonderful."

"Yes, daughter, they were."

Wisdom of the Ancients *was written for a 500-word limit competition run jointly by Wattpad and National Geographic on the theme of "Planet or Plastic". There were over 5500 entries and Wisdom was picked for one of the top 10 entries in the judging in February 2019, though missed out on first place. In May 2020 it suddenly found itself at the number one spot of the Wattpad Science Fiction chart. At the time of writing (November 2021) it is still in the top 10 and has a habit of popping back up to number one every so often. You can see the original here along with all the comments on it:*

https://www.wattpad.com/652804505-wisdom-of-the-ancients

The End